ETERNAL LOVE AND PROTECTION

EJ TAYLOR

This book is dedicated to my parents for their support and my grandparents for their wisdom.

Prologue

The man woke to the alarm. The noise was familiar but hadn't made complete sense for the first few seconds.

It was then that the rolling smoke came to view.

There were no words, only sudden panic and instant sweat. His wife lay peacefully beside him. He shook her vigorously. She woke, saw the smoke and screamed for her child. He stood and lifted her forcefully over his shoulder.

'You know I'll get him!' he shouted.

He ploughed down the stairs and placed her outside the front door.

The heat and smoke went unnoticed as he returned to the upper floor towards the child's bedroom. The screaming mother added an extra element of speed to his actions. The alarm continued to bellow forcefully.

The flames were now towering and crawling across the ceiling. He ran down the small corridor to the boy's room and burst through the door. The room was still clear, the child sleeping peacefully.

'Thank god.' He fell to his knees.

The sound of his wife's screams lifted him to his feet and drove him forward. He lifted the boy gently, keeping the blanket wrapped around his small body. The child stirred.

'It's OK. Go back to sleep,' the father spoke gently.

As he escaped the corridor, he turned to flames leaping up through the staircase. The mother let out another wild scream once the two were in view from the frame of the front door. Her hand was outstretched in terror.

This woke the boy, and now he became alert to the situation.

'Daddy?' he cried as he observed the hellish inferno.

'It's OK, son. It's OK. I will look after you. Nothing will ever happen to you while I'm here.'

The boy seemed calmed, but cried silently in fear.

He wrapped the boy into a tighter cocoon with the blanket and lifted him above head height. He ran swiftly down the collapsing staircase, through the burning flames. As the ground beneath his feet rapidly deteriorated, he reached the front door and thrust the boy into the mother's arms.

Her screams quietened to a whimper.

The man threw himself to the ground and rolled to remove the fire that had caught him during the dash. It cleared rapidly, but his mind was detached from any bodily damage he may have incurred. He looked up to see the mother checking her child for any damage.

Sirens in the background became apparent.

He rushed over to the mother and child and hugged them together. 'We'll be OK. I'll make sure of that. I will always watch over my family – always.'

Chapter One

It was a glorious day. Robert Turner sat on his lush green grass, watching the birds drink from a small puddle left from the torrential rain just a few hours before. He could hear the young school kids in the distance playing on the field; it reminded him of those typical summer days that everybody celebrated. He was demonstrating his love and worship of the sun by facing its direction, with his eyes shut. He grinned with obvious pleasure.

A faint female voice grew louder. 'Rob, babe? Rob! When you gonna come in 'n' help me with this damn thing?'

Robert didn't want to break this feeling. It didn't come around very often these days, so he didn't respond.

She mumbled under her breath and disappeared back up the patio into the large, double-doored entrance to the rear of the house.

Robert could hear her slamming things around in distinct frustration. He tried not to let his conscience get the better of him. He'd always been the 'soft-hearted' type who wouldn't say no to helping anyone.

This time, however, was his time. All Robert wanted was one quiet afternoon of relaxation with the bonus of a few rays touching his sun-deprived skin. The harder he tried to fight his conscience, the less he could relax.

She thinks I'm asleep. I'll get away with it. I can help her with the program tonight, after dinner, Rob thought, as he managed to keep his position on the grass until hunger got the better of him.

The house was spacious, with marble flooring through the main corridors. In the lounge was a large, black-leathered three-piece suite. The walls throughout the house were a clinical white.

The lady was sat in the kitchen, humped over a keyboard, trying to read a book just within arm's length.

Robert walked quietly through to the end of the vast length of the kitchen, where he could see his wife's long, soft hair. His footsteps were silent as he crept behind. During this short walk, he admired the golden locks, flowing down her slender back.

'How's it going there, hun?'

She turned to face him. 'How does it look like it's going? I've been here all day, while you've sat sunning yourself in half-damp grass!'

Her face was flushed with frustration and anger. Her big brown eyes looked black with rage. Robert moved to a chair behind her.

'Come on, hun. You know I don't get much time to relax. I'm here now though, so let's see if I can be of service.'

They both sat in silence as Rob searched through the book for a short cut to understanding the program. As time passed, the light of the computer monitor grew brighter. And as darkness fell, Rob had explained the complete package in simple terms.

Claire was comforted by the company and tuition. At least now she could go to work in the morning knowing how to store information in the in-house program. Just two days ago, her boss had requested that all staff take the new package home to study, claiming that it would only take up a couple of hours of every-one's time.

Claire hated computers and knew other people from her department grasped new systems much quicker than she did. As she cringed over this, she calmly asked, 'Why do things have to keep changing?'

A grin appeared on Robert's face as he reached over and gently kissed her on the cheek. He stroked her gentle jaw line on one side and slowly got up to walk back through to the lounge area.

'I'd better take Jack out for a bit. Don't want 'im crapping everywhere!'

Claire acknowledged his comment with a nod, as she switched the computer off and tidied the area.

When Robert came to the lounge, the young Alsatian had sprawled himself out on the leather sofa.

'Oi, Jack! You'd better get your friggin' arse off there before your mum sees you!'

He gently pulled Jack down and led him outdoors. They both walked as best buddies down the front path that led to a small, one-lane road. Robert's hunger had been completely forgotten with all of the distractions. The pair crossed the road and disappeared into the darkness of the park ahead.

In the meantime, Claire Turner decided to prepare two glasses of white wine and carried them upstairs.

Once in the bedroom, she placed them together on a large, bedside table. She stripped off her clothing and slipped into a thin, pink dressing gown. She took a hairbrush and watched in the mirror as her hair flowed with each stroke she made.

Claire loved her hair. At the young age of thirty-five, it was her greatest feature – long and blonde, with the odd natural kink in it. It was still her natural colour, with shine that never appeared to fade.

She did her best to keep a youthful look, always pampering herself with facemasks and facials and sticking to a low-calorie and low-fat diet. It was not obvious that there was a seven-year difference between her and Robert.

She did her best to keep herself the way she did. Robert was a young, athletic and attractive man. 'Quite a catch,' her friends said. At twenty-eight, he was an all-round talent; a computer genius, with the looks of a film star and the body of a Greek god.

Claire was so proud at her wedding. She'd found the tall, dark and handsome man she'd always dreamt of. Her marriage was still at the tender age of two years, although she'd known him for five.

Everything seemed too good to be true for the first few months. Once she'd experienced the usual problems of relationships and marriage, she realised that looks and skills weren't the be-all and end-all.

A frown appeared on her face as she wondered what was holding her husband up.

The longer she waited, the more she reminisced about the good days.

A sudden feeling of confusion and a strange emotion of sadness appeared.

★

Robert had turned a corner after a few trees. Jack had run ahead as always, hunting for any small creature that could be chased.

'Jack!' Robert raised both hands to either side of his mouth in an attempt to throw his voice further.

The dog had gone out of Robert's view. It wasn't unusual, but it was best to bring Jack back close occasionally to know he was still safe.

Squinting in the dark, Robert noticed another person close by.

Must be another dog walker, or some weirdo looking for a place to drink 'n' sleep he thought.

It didn't feel comfortable to shout now, with someone directly ahead.

The figure had a familiar shape. It didn't seem to alter direction, just headed straight towards Robert.

Adrenaline ran through him now. It wasn't a comfortable scenario.

'Shit,' Robert whispered. He felt a slight tinge of panic, wondering why he hadn't realised the risks of walking through a quiet park in the dark before leaving the house. He looked at the figure, knowing it was male, but trying to prepare for any situation.

Where was Jack, damn it! Hopefully the bloke would pass straight by.

He was close now, with no intention of changing course. The air felt tense. Robert held his fists ready for any physical situation. He could feel his heart racing as he wondered why the man didn't speak or move over to the side to pass. Robert tried diverting to the side in order to walk past, but the figure moved front-on, charging directly towards him.

'He-hello?' A nervous stammer came out for the first time in his adult life.

Suddenly, from the left, came hammering footsteps. He glanced sideways, expecting to see an accomplice.

It was Jack!

Get 'im, boy! was his instant thought.

He turned to find a clear view ahead. The figure had gone!

Robert spun 180 degrees, his eyes moving fast to work out where the person had disappeared to. Adrenaline hit him again.

'Come on, boy.' He tried to say it calmly as he swiftly attached Jack's lead to his collar.

Claire sat on the bed, sipping her wine, when a sweaty forehead appeared through the gap of the bedroom door. She stood.

'Where the hell have you been? I nearly sent a search party out!'

'I'm really sorry, hun. I thought I'd give Jack a good run tonight.'

'Shh-ure. Sometimes I wonder who takes priority in this house.'

A disappointed look appeared on Robert's face. He felt as if his efforts hadn't been appreciated.

'I can tell you let the alcohol keep you company while I was out anyway. You've got work early tomorrow. You're gonna look like shit. I'm going for a shower. Some of us take our responsibilities seriously.'

Her attitude changed. She slumped on the bed, head hanging, too intoxicated to argue. When Robert was angry, he didn't leave room for discussion. From her experience, he said his piece, then walked away. In this case he went towards the ensuite to clean up, ready for bed.

Chapter Two

Maria Jackson sat at her workstation, staring at the computer screen ahead.

Thoughts were running through her head as she sat, trying to look attentive. Her boss sat only a few yards away from her, which meant her daydreaming had to be shielded by an expression of concentration.

Luckily, this came naturally to her.

Maria enjoyed her early start, avoiding traffic, people rushing into the offices, the chatter and disruptions. She got more done in the first two hours of peace than the subsequent six.

Today, she knew she wasn't going to get much done. She'd helped her friend through a depressing time the night before and now worry had set in.

The first three hours flew by due to her well-hidden dream state. A saddened face approached her desk. The familiar look brought Maria to her senses.

'Do you think he noticed me sneak in?' the familiar voice asked.

'Na. You look like crap, though. I'd stay out the way today if I were you. I'll cover for ya.'

'Cheers, buddy. I'll try and get the paperwork done, then nowt'll be said.'

Claire Turner walked slowly to her paper-cluttered desk. Maria always covered for her.

What a buddy, she thought. *I don't know how she puts up with me. I wish she'd have a problem, just to return all the favours.*

Picking up the paperwork, she keyed in the figures. Luckily, the new in-house program was remembered, and by the end of the day she'd worked through it as if she'd been using it for years.

The time moved fast and the occasional glance from Maria comforted her.

Robert Turner had finished work early in order to get to his local boxing gym before the mass influx at six o'clock in the evening. His fists were hitting a large, heavy, leather bag. His training partner, Richard James, held the opposite side to inhibit the swinging movement. Both had trained together since the age of thirteen.

Richard had been bullied by the largest boy in his class prior to his decision to train. Every day for a whole year, the large boy would push him, kick his shins or spit in his face.

Richard never had his revenge, but was feared by the large boy as soon as word had spread about the boxing lessons.

Richard had asked Robert to join the club with him. Once there, the addiction took them to various bouts and their bodies grew strong. Nobody attempted to push their luck with the pair. They were as close as brothers and grew up together.

Richard was a slightly shorter, stockier man than Robert. Their birthdays were only a couple of months apart. They currently shared the same age of twenty-eight years. Richard, however, looked a little older.

His hair had begun receding at the tender age of twenty-one. He soon rectified the expected self-image, by shaving his head regularly. Ego was his middle name, unlike Robert, who had the natural humility of a Shaolin monk.

Robert was now punching the bag a little more aggressively, as he remembered his close call last night.

They both walked away from the bag as if it was a practised, synchronised move.

'So, bro. You know I know, so you know you may as well tell me.' Richard spoke with a side glance.

'Yeah, I knew you'd see it. I was gonna tell you, but was hoping to train first.'

Richard wiped the sweat off his forehead with the strapping around his hands, slowly unwrapped one hand, then the other. There was a controlled silence.

'Well,' Richard started, 'last night was pretty friggin' freaky. I was walking Jack around quite late, when this bloke walked straight at me. I thought he was gonna pull a knife on me or something, but when Jack reappeared from the dark and he disappeared. I looked around for a bit, then legged it back.'

'Was he a drunk or a tramp?'

'Well, that's what I thought, but he must've been a quick drunk bloke, 'cause when Jack appeared, he didn't hang around.'

'You got home though! I don't think you should go there again in the dark, man.' He looked at Robert with one raised eyebrow.

'Yeah. If Claire finds out, she'd go mental. Luckily for me, she was too intoxicated to even care.'

Richard looked even more concerned. 'Aah, man! Why can't she lay off the drink for five minutes? You should get a fit bird, like mine.'

'Claire *is* a fit bird; she's just not liking work at the mo. I think the drink helps her relax,' Robert replied convincingly.

'You know my thoughts on that, Rob. I know the drinking is a new hobby from what I can see, but it's gonna be a descending spiral!'

'Yep. I'll have a word, I reckon – catch it early. Anyway, I'm hitting the showers. I don't want another excuse for moans when I get home.'

Robert walked away, picked up a small white towel and flung it over his shoulder. Richard loosened one shoelace on a low stool, watching him.

Robert walked into the shower and turned the water on; he enjoyed the feel of it running through his hair and down his body. All the tension from training was instantly released. The water was lukewarm, the way he liked it – much more refreshing than a hot shower, he always stressed to others.

He enjoyed the sensation for a few moments, then massaged the soap over his body. As he rinsed, he reminisced about some raunchy moments with his wife, Claire. It made him want to hurry home and see the lady he loved.

Quickly drying and dressing, he walked back through to the main gym area. The boxing ring was almost central, with punching bags of various sizes dotted around the hall. Rich must've gone, he thought, as he noticed his bag was no longer present. I couldn't have been that long, surely!

Robert left the gym and ensured the front door catch had secured the building as it closed behind him.

The warm sun was on his face as he walked down the main path that would lead him home. The road nearby was quiet and the pavement ahead was bare, peaceful.

After a while he could see his driveway appear in the distance. Her car wasn't there. Always late home these days! He frowned, his dark eyes looking even darker.

As Robert opened his front door, the large Alsatian jumped up to greet him. Huge paws landed on his shoulders as Robert rubbed either side of Jack's neck, feeling the loose flesh in his hands and the warm breath in his face.

'Come on, let's go out.' Robert gently lowered Jack and walked with him to the rear doors of the house to allow the poor dog some toilet duties.

They both eventually settled down in front of the television like two best friends.

Time passed and Robert awoke to darkness and a blaring advertisement on the TV. He glanced at the dog, who was still sleeping comfortably, snoring faintly. His paws were underneath his body and his head on Robert's lap.

A distinct bang came from the ceiling above. *Claire's home*, he thought.

He walked to the large bay window at the front of the house and peaked through the horizontal blinds.

The car's not there! Maybe she put it in for service and grabbed a lift home.

Claire's work was a twenty-minute drive away.

'Claire?' he shouted, still standing in the dark with the glare of the television.

There was no reply.

The dog stirred, but continued to lie comfortably.

'Well, some guard dog you—' his sentence ended early as a second thud sounded from above his head.

Jack remained still, undisturbed.

Robert decided to grit his teeth and investigate. The whole house was in complete darkness, which instantly confused him. He grabbed his baseball bat, which was always kept behind the front door of the house. There were two possibilities: Claire had either crept to bed in a drunken state, or it was an intruder.

Despite his dislike for Claire's drinking problem, he hoped it was the former.

He nervously switched the stair lights on and climbed the stairs as light-footed as possible.

As soon as he reached the top, he reached to switch the landing light on. The hairs at the back of his neck stood on end as he veered to the right, heading towards their bedroom.

He felt a cool breeze drift past him as he reached the door. As he entered, he reached for the light switch. Brightness flooded the room, and he instantly noticed the curtains blowing inward.

He walked in and quietly closed the window. On his approach, he looked down to see a fallen picture.

Well, that would explain one of the thuds, I guess!

He decided not to pick it up until the whole house had been patrolled and it wasn't until the house was clear in his own mind that he decided to place the only fallen object back in its original position.

Looking at the picture, he sat on his bed, reminiscing.

Robert and his father had been for an outing. They'd been to an air show on a boiling hot day. Both had red faces from the sun and were leaning on a stationed plane for the pose.

God, I miss you, he thought, as tried to shake the images of his dead father. It still hurt to think that five years ago his dad had passed away following a tragic car accident.

His mother, Jude, was the independent type anyway, so quickly adjusted to widowed life.

Robert watched over her in a subtle way so as not to appear too obsessive. He was always close to his mother and did his best in his adult life to protect her. He'd regularly check that she was OK physically, emotionally and financially. It was done in subtle, observational methods. Although he knew that she knew, nothing was ever said.

As he returned to the present, he heard the familiar engine sound pull into his drive.

What had taken her so long?

He raced downstairs to get to the front door. As he opened it, he saw the face of an unhappy wife.

'OK, I don't want to aggravate anything, but where the hell have you been?'

Claire walked straight past, not even thinking to close the front door behind her. As she walked towards the kitchen, she explained.

'The boss called a meeting. I did try calling, but it just rang. I thought you must be at the gym and I had to go in. I hope you weren't worried.'

'And you didn't get another chance to call or at least leave a message on the answering machine?'

'Well, I guess I thought you wouldn't give a shit anyway, after last night.'

Robert closed the front door gently and walked over to her. She now faced him, leaning against a worktop in the kitchen. His voice changed to a whisper.

'Hun, last night was last night. We've had bad times before, but never left each other in the dark. So which one is it? You either hoped I wouldn't worry or hoped I didn't give a shit?'

'Oh, Rob! I'm tired. I can't be bothered to argue tonight.'

'Babes, I'm just afraid I'm gonna lose you.' He walked towards her and held her gently by her waist, looking compassionately into her eyes.

They stood in silence for what seemed a few minutes. Robert gently touched the top button of her blouse and cautiously unfastened it, waiting for a negative reaction.

As nothing was said, he continued to unbutton her blouse and slid one hand under one side of the material. He gently caressed her breast.

Pleasant moans were leaving Claire's lips as Robert continued to massage and hold her close.

She reciprocated and untied the belt of his trousers, placing her hand deep inside.

He picked her up onto the worktop and aggressively entered her.

★

Matthew Carter sat in his darkened lounge, holding a large mug of coffee in one hand and a small photo in the other. Light music played in the distance. *Not long now*, he thought.

His lounge consisted of one large, black leather sofa and one large coffee table parallel to it, within arm's reach. He had no television, only a small stereo system with speakers either side that were floor to ceiling.

Matthew leant over to place his mug on the table. There were piles of paper spread in front of him. He placed the small photo among them.

A muffled phone ring became apparent, which made Matthew sit bolt upright. He pulled a small silver phone from his trouser pocket, briefly glancing at the caller's number. Pressing a button, he placed the phone to his ear.

'Matt?' a powerful male voice asked.

'Yeah.' The reply was very relaxed.

'Matt, I know you don't want me to know, but could you just convince me that it's all for a good cause?'

'I told you before, Chris. I don't do anything without checking it out first. All you have to worry about is taking the dosh. It's a good deal for a small job. You help me, I help you.'

'OK. I guess I'm just getting a bit nervous. Sorry.'

Matthew knew it wasn't such a good idea getting a kid to do the job, but he just needed a simple job doing, and he knew the youth would do anything for more than the usual pay packet.

'Look, it's a one-minute job. Just think about the reward at the end. Have you decided what you're gonna do with it?'

There was a brief pause, but the breathing down the phone confirmed Chris was still on the line. 'Well… I think I'm gonna take my babe and go somewhere hot.'

Chapter Three

It was Sunday. Robert and Claire had woken late morning. Still in bed, Robert rolled over towards her.

'Hun?' he asked quietly, 'do you mind if I do the usual? I won't stay as long this time.'

Claire turned slowly to face him. 'I never stop you from seeing your mum. You know that.'

'Yeah. I just wondered if you'd like to come this time. You haven't seen her for about a month now.'

Claire's eyes were wide open as she faced him. 'I told you why: it's awkward. She just talks to you and completely ignores me, so what's the point?'

'She's just a bit down sometimes. She sounded more lively the other day.' Robert's voice was convincing.

Claire rolled to the edge of her side of the bed and reached for her dressing gown. As she sat up, her tone of voice changed to a stern one.

'Rob, I understand that you need to see your mum on Sundays and I'll always give you that time. You're lucky you still have a mum around; you've got to make the most of her. The problem is that I know for a fact that she doesn't want to see me. If she invites me next time, then I'll come, OK?'

Claire walked away, wrapping the cotton belt around her waist.

He heard her descend the stairs as he slowly climbed out of bed and dressed himself.

One day we'll wake up to pleasantries, he thought.

Suddenly, a deep growl, overshadowed by a high-pitched scream, came from downstairs.

Robert, still barefooted, ran downstairs to find Jack confining Claire to a corner of the kitchen. The dog's upper lips were raised and twitching, revealing large, threatening teeth. His eyes were threatening to kill, as he sensed Claire's fear.

'Jack! Jack! Come here, damn it! Jack!'

Claire suddenly became aware of Robert's powerful voice, but couldn't move an inch for fear of aggravation. She noticed the dog suddenly getting dragged backwards. From its mouth came a small yelp.

A concerned face came towards her a few seconds later.

'Honey? Are you OK?' Robert noticed her pale face and rigid appearance.

'I-I-I only came into the kitchen for a drink.' Her voice was shaky.

He hugged her and felt the shivers slowly calm.

After a few minutes, he asked, 'Are you sure you didn't provoke him in any way?'

As soon as she spoke, he knew it was the wrong question. 'Rob! I told you! I just walked into the kitchen! I didn't even acknowledge the little shit!'

The dog barked in the background.

'OK, I just needed to know. Usually there's a trigger for these kind of things.'

'Rob, did you lock the damn thing away? I don't want him in the house! He could've killed me!'

Robert began to realise the consequences. His best buddy was going to be taken away from him.

She continued, 'I mean, I know he's your dog, but if he's gonna fucking attack me like that, then he needs putting down.'

'Right. The best thing I can do for now is keep him in the garden in his kennel. In the meantime, I guess I'm gonna have to find another owner.'

Claire turned to rinse a cup in the sink, then headed for the staircase. As she left, she shouted, 'He'd better be gone by the end of the day! It's my home too!'

Robert stood with his head in his hands.

Chapter Four

It was Monday morning. Robert left early to get to the office before the traffic had built up. Claire had decided to take the week off work to sort a few things out at home.

The doorbell went.

Claire walked over to see who it was, although she had a pretty good idea. On opening the door, she viewed a smaller man than she had imagined.

'Mrs Turner?' He looked slightly nervous.

'Yes. Come on in. The beast is in the lounge. If you go through that door there...' she pointed. 'In the meantime, I'll just lock myself in the kitchen. Could you let me know when you've done?'

'Sure, Mrs Turner. My name is Philip. My colleague, Sally, is just on her way.'

'Right. Well, I'll just disappear into this room. I'll get you a drink afterwards if you fancy one.'

Claire walked briskly to the kitchen and closed herself in.

Philip stood still, looking a fraction concerned.

This man had learnt to trust animals more than humans in his experience as a vet. He was very much in touch with nature. His genteel characteristics matched his small frame and amiable facial features.

'Phil! I'm coming!'

A thin, young, blonde-haired lady ran up the driveway with a small briefcase in one hand. He turned to face her with a grin. She studied his expression and asked, 'So, what's wrong with this one?'

'All I know is that he's suddenly become very nasty towards the lady owner and for no reason. They've requested that he be put down.'

Sally looked glum. 'Ah... well, can't I add him to my collection?'

'You know the rules, Sal. Let's take a look at him.'

Sally had a farm full of cats, rabbits and dogs that had been neglected by people. She'd then sell them on to people, who'd have to go through her rigid vetting processes.

They walked quietly into the lounge area and called the dog's name to test its first reaction.

Jack looked up from a lying position. He'd been locked either outside or in the lounge for a few hours now and had become very remorseful. Phil could see these feelings at a simple glance.

'Shit, I hate these ones. I bet she did something to cause retaliation. I mean, look at him.'

Sally signalled Philip to silence with one finger over her lips, '*Shhh*. Don't let the lady hear. You don't know how nasty he may have been towards her.'

Philip hesitantly took hold of the briefcase and felt inside for a fresh packet of needles. He felt sick as he thought about ending such a beautiful animal's life.

'Give it to me.' Sally reached to take his items, when suddenly she was pushed to the floor by a hand larger than any she'd ever felt or seen. Dazed and confused, she looked up to see why Phil had been so physical.

'Are you OK?' Phil asked with an even more confused look on his face.

'What did you do that for?' She pulled herself back to her feet.

'Do what? You just fell back on your bum. Did you lose your balance?'

Sally felt silly and thought she must've fallen after all, as Phil couldn't have pushed her from the direction he was facing. Confused, she tried to prepare the injection.

Again, a flash of a figure pushed a huge open palm into her chest, forcing her to the ground.

The large thud made Phil rush to her assistance. 'What on earth is wrong with you? I thought I was the one with the problem!'

'I, uh, don't understand. Someone keeps pushing me over.'

Philip didn't quite know how to respond. He took the items from Sally's hands. 'I think you should stay there until you feel better. I'll take care of this.'

Sally sat in mystification. Her face became sweaty and pale. As Philip prepared the injection, he wondered if he should be taking care of Sally first. He took a brief look at her and decided that he'd be in much more trouble if he caused the death of a human rather than an animal.

The ambulance came and took Sally away. Philip stood by the front door, apologising to his client. He asked Claire if she'd mind a visit later on in the day, to give him time to check on Sally and arrange for another assistant. She agreed to an early afternoon visit.

Just as soon as Claire had said goodbye to the vet, she heard the phone ring. She closed the door and went to answer it.

'Hello?' she answered innocently.

'Claire! What's going on? Rich just called me at work to say there's an ambulance outside the house.'

'Oh, hello, Rob. That friend of yours is a nosy bugger. Tell him to get a life. It's nothing.'

'I'm coming home! I've got a lot to talk to you about. First the vet and then an ambulance?'

Claire's blood began to boil. 'What did you do? Send a spy out, Rob? Can't you just do your job and forget about me for one minute?'

'I've had enough of this. I know what you're up to. I told you I'd find a good home for Jack. If he's hurt at all, I swear I'll—'

'You'll what? That dog could've killed me, Rob! Maybe you should just take him and leave. You care more about him than you do me!'

'How can you say that? How could you throw us away just like that?' His voice turned to a loud whisper. 'I'm coming home. We'll discuss this later.'

With that, Rob replaced the receiver. His team leader hovered over him. Robert looked vexed.

'Sorry, Mike. I've got a bit of a problem at home. Do you mind if I pop over there for five? You know I don't normally do this kind of thing.'

Mike always carried an adamant expression with a voice to match, but his voice was considerate this time. 'Sure. I've never seen you like this. You'd better sort it out and come back with an eased mind.'

Robert grabbed his thin jacket and walked out of his office as if he was about to tackle a bull. Colleagues turned their heads in curiosity, almost like a domino effect as he walked down the corridor.

He climbed into his car and screeched the tires as he pulled away. Most days Robert would walk to work, as he was only a few minutes' walk away, but as Claire was at home he thought it'd be nice to get use of the shared car.

He pulled into the driveway, leapt out of the car and entered the house. Claire got up nervously from a seated position in the kitchen. She had been sat on a swivel chair, talking to a friend on her mobile phone.

'Can we talk about this calmly?' she asked.

Robert calmed down when he realised she looked slightly afraid. He stood slightly round-shouldered with his arms by his side.

'I'm not gonna hurt you. You know that. It's just… you know how much I love that dog. I don't know what triggered his reaction, but surely that's not justification for murder. I'm giving him to Rich. He'll give him a good home. Just promise me I can go to work without worrying about you tryin' to kill him again.'

Claire walked over and flung her arms around him. Her eyes filled with tears as she felt his emotions. 'I'm so sorry! I should have thought about your feelings for Jack. I was so shocked and annoyed that an animal made me feel threatened in my own home. I didn't really think of anyone but myself. I'm really sorry, Rob. I promise not to do anything.'

Robert's expression changed to a thoughtful one. *Something weird is going on here*, he thought.

'Look,' he found himself saying, 'I have to get back to work, but when I come back, I'll take Jack over to Richard's, then we can forget this whole thing ever happened. OK?'

Claire loosened her arms slightly and leant back to see his face. 'This is all my fault. I don't know what I did to upset Jack, but if I wasn't here you'd still have him around.'

'Come on. I don't know what you're trying to say, but we love each other and have done for a while now. Jack has to respect both of us if he's going to live under this roof. If you're unhappy, then so am I. He'll be going to a good home, as I say. I can still see him and take him for walks. He'll just have a new owner. I can still be his friend.'

'You're amazing.'

Robert acknowledged the brief reply, then suddenly remembered work. 'Babes, I gotta go before I lose my job. There's a major deadline for a new program I've gotta set up.'

Claire took her arms away and sat down again.

Robert looked at her, confused.

'Don't go all cold on me, babes. I wouldn't mind a proper goodbye kiss to feed me for the afternoon. We can chat more when I get home.'

Claire physically responded. They walked to the front door together. Rob walked ahead to the car, his face still in her direction.

'See you later, hun. I'm glad we've kind of sorted things out. Oh, and by the way – I didn't get Rich to spy. He was more concerned about the ambulance, but couldn't see the connection to the vet arriving earlier.'

'OK. I guessed you didn't have anything to do with it and that Rich was just doing his concerned neighbour thing. I was just using it as ammunition for our argument. Sorry. Now get to work, you!'

She walked in and picked up the phone with the intention of cancelling the vet arrangement.

Chapter Five

Richard James held his glass up. Three other glasses clinked together in the pub, almost synchronised.

'Drink up, boys 'n' girls!'

The four took reasonable sips from their drinks, then placed them down on the table. Richard placed his free hand on the lap of his lady friend and gave her a cheeky grin. He looked across at Robert and gently spoke over the table. 'Rob, I promise to take good care of Jack. You aint got nothing to worry about, man.'

Robert gave a knowing smile. 'I know that. I would only have given him to you.'

The two men clashed their glasses together again. The two ladies looked slightly awkward.

Claire had not met Rachael before, but knew she'd be a beauty. Richard always found the 'hot' ladies. Unfortunately, to date, the personalities hadn't matched. He always seemed to find the ladies they classed as 'psycho'. Robert and Claire would always give his new discoveries a fair chance to prove otherwise.

Rachael had the expected high cheek bones, long blonde hair, a tall, slim figure and make-up that looked professionally done. She could have been Miss World. Claire thought that the light may have enhanced her looks that evening, as she began to compare herself.

'So, Rachael, how did you meet this chump?' Robert asked with such dignity.

Rachael looked surprised that she'd been asked a question. She was about to answer when Richard jumped in. 'I found this beauty when she came to our gym looking for some training.' He hugged her expressively.

'So,' Robert replied, 'you want to box? A pretty little thing like you?' He turned to wink at Claire, just to comfort any thoughts of deliberate flirtation.

'Well…' she attempted to reply.

'Actually,' Richard jumped in again, 'she was hoping we'd have them classes in box aerobics. You know, the non-contact workout with the boxin' moves?' He grinned proudly.

Robert nodded. 'We're a bit spit 'n' sawdust, aint we, Rich?'

'Yeah, but the cool thing is, she wants to come an' have a go at the tough stuff. I convinced 'er that we wear the padding and we'll bring some more girls in for her to practise with.'

Both men glanced at Claire at the same time.

'Don't look at me!' she shouted, with a look of horror on her face. 'You know I'm the soft, flower-arranging type.'

Richard threw a cheeky look at Robert and added, 'Well, so's Rob, an' he doesn't lose every fight.'

Robert just pointed a confident index finger in his direction. Claire thought it'd be her chance to get a sentence over to Rachael. 'Just don't get like these guys. Sometimes I wonder if they have any life other than the boxing one.'

A double 'oooh' came from both men, as they were about to take sips from their glasses.

'Rob's got a fight this weekend. This is one of the top amateur fighters in his division. If he beats this guy, he may be on his way to stardom, babe.' Richard directed the words at Claire.

'Well, we'll see. That'll mean no action for me Saturday night, then!' Claire sipped her drink to hide her sudden embarrassment. Claire often spoke her mind, with regret following only a second behind.

Rachael let out a quiet giggle. Richard held her across the shoulders again and pulled her closer.

The drinks flowed and the conversation eased as time flew by.

The two couples left at closing time, giggling and staggering towards the taxi they'd arranged only a few minutes before.

Claire and Robert arrived home and walked through to the lounge area. Robert suddenly felt sad at the sudden realisation of having no best friend to greet him at the door.

'I know, hun.' Claire seemed to read his mind. She kissed him on the lips and hugged him.

They slowly made their way upstairs, still arms wrapped around each other.

Chapter Six

Robert regretted drinking on an evening during the week. Claire still slept as he picked up his prepared clothes from the chair at the side of the bed. He crept to the car without checking his state in the mirror.

Claire was rudely awoken by the telephone ringing.

'Hello?' She managed to speak fairly clearly.

The caller spoke for a while. Claire listened with a thin, contented smile.

'OK. Well, if you get a free lunch, let me know.' She leant to put the phone down. There was another pause. 'Just let me know when it's done, OK?' She spoke her final words, then replaced the phone.

Claire pulled herself out of bed, tied her hair back and put some casual clothes on.

As she walked downstairs she noticed the dirt marks on the banister and dog hairs on the floor.

She walked towards the kitchen, opened the fridge and gulped a large quantity of milk.

She spotted the vacuum cleaner and aimed for it.

Claire vacuumed and polished the entire house, then managed to clean the kitchen and bathroom before collapsing in a heap on the lounge sofa. She lazily picked up the remote control and switched the television on.

Before she had chance to adjust to the programme, there was a loud knock at the front door.

'Ah, come on!' she moaned, deciding not to rise from her comfortable position.

The doorbell sounded. Claire wondered if the person on the other side had heard her moan. Her worry faded as she decided to stick to her decision to ignore the visitor.

She looked at the clock and noticed that time had passed fairly rapidly during her cleaning frenzy. It was now lunchtime.

Then the phone now rang.

'What the f—?' She stopped herself from the profanity.

Again, Claire decided to ignore the invasion of her moment of peace. She gazed at the television, when suddenly a familiar figure appeared at the front window, trying to look in.

'Dam it, Rob! Can't I have a day off without you always being about?' she complained, as she knew her expected peace was now a distant hope.

She opened the door to a grinning expression. 'Hun? I thought I'd surprise you and spend a little lunch time with you.' He presented a large pizza box.

'Ah!' Her mood suddenly improved. 'My flavour or yours?'

They normally argued over which pizza toppings to go for. Claire was always partial to the vegetarian option, which Robert opposed with the meaty version.

'Well, you know these days you can get both styles on the same pizza. I took control and ordered a half 'n' half. One half is my lovely meaty, spicy one. Your half is the cheese, tomato, onion and sweetcorn one.' He sounded as if he'd read an advertisement script.

She rolled her eyes, smiling. 'Well, thanks, darl. I need a good feed. I just scrubbed the place to death. The place was a tip again.'

'It couldn't have been that bad,' he said regretfully, as he noticed the sudden challenge in her eyes. 'Actually, we haven't touched it for a few days, so I guess it was in desperate need of doing. Well done, babe,' he quickly added.

She remained silent as she took a couple of plates from a cupboard above her head.

'So. What were you planning to do with the rest of your day?' he asked uncomfortably.

'Well, I thought I'd just laze in front of the TV. I'll be even lazier once I've eaten this.'

Robert now wished he'd had the same week off.

'You know I've got my latest project to do at the mo?' he asked.

She suddenly gave Robert her full attention. 'Yeah.'

He helped her to divide the pizzas on the plates in the hope of distracting her.

'Well, it looks as if I'll be doing some long hours to get it all done in a fortnight. It's gonna be a tight deadline!' he said dramatically to exaggerate the foreseen tension of the workload.

She looked down at the food and handed a plate to him. As she lifted hers and walked towards the lounge area, she sat with the expectancy of his following. He complied with her obvious hint and sat opposite her, hoping of a positive response to his announcement.

'Well, you've worked late many times before, so I'm sure I can handle two weeks of it,' she said, before beginning her first mouthful of pizza.

'I have to be honest with you, you know that. It's just that it could be really late. I'm talking early-in-the-morning starts to early-in-the-morning finishes!'

'So, what about your training? I thought you had a fight soon. Training usually comes first with you.'

He looked very guilty at this stage.

'Well, that's the thing. We're hardly gonna see each other. I'll be leaving at, say, eight o'clock in the morning, training at lunchtimes, then coming home at a silly time. I will do my best to be back home shortly after midnight to see you before you sleep and so I won't get too buggered.'

'Well,' she started. 'You're crazy, but I guess I've heard worse.'

He looked sad for a moment. 'It's just that everything's come at once and I'm trying to keep everyone happy.'

No sympathy came from Claire. 'Well, these things happen. We can catch up when it's over. I just hope you get some kind of result from it, that's all.'

That was enough to convince Robert that Claire had accepted the situation.

'OK, well, I hope the next couple of weeks go quickly. I'm just gonna miss you, and I'm frightened that you'll go a little cold. I just want you to know that I may need your support more than ever. Sorry to get sloppy.'

Claire glanced across, looking slightly concerned. 'Don't worry, hun. It'll be OK. I didn't realise you were that worried.'

He placed his plate on the floor and came over to her. 'Thanks, babes. Just hearing those words from you means a hell of a lot.' He reached over and kissed her on the forehead. 'I'd better make a move now. If you want the rest of my pizza, it's all yours! I'll catch you when I get in. I'm easin' into it tonight, so I should be home by about eleven.'

Claire followed Robert with her eyes to the front door. He walked with a dragged pace, as if he had to force himself away from home.

The front door closed and Claire retired to her previous comfortable position and ate until she felt slightly uncomfortable.

Chapter Seven

Robert sat at his desk. The lights around him now appeared dim as the external darkness set in. The floor plan had the typical office style. Every 'section' had four large desks, with a computer, monitor and keyboard on each. Each floor was spacious. The building was full of staff employed by the same company. With ten floors of people and equipment, 'DAGEN' was a reputable company to work for. The company name comes from the two words – Data Genius – with the nature of the business being to create databases for other large companies. As with all large companies, there were various departments.

Robert felt privileged to work in the heart of the concept. He worked on the development of original programs. Ninety-nine per cent of the time, his original ideas and complete packages were approved and praised by highly respected members of the company. Robert was constantly rewarded financially. Bonuses came through so frequently that he planned his finances in expectation of them.

Tonight Robert started a fresh challenge. He had been told of the possibility of promotion if this new program was successful. Robert was the type of person who would put all of his efforts into work or a hobby. A favourite motto of his was 'If you're gonna do something, do it properly.' His friends and family always thought of him as a perfectionist, though there was an element of worry over whether or not he sometimes did a little bit too much. To date he had proved them wrong.

It was now nine o'clock at night. He looked small among the desks and equipment. He only knew of two other people in the building: the security staff. One security person had already walked past him three times. The first time, a comment was made. Robert thought that maybe they must be a little bored. He didn't reply for fear of starting a conversation he wouldn't have time for.

As he typed and concentrated, he suddenly realised he was a little thirsty.

Time for a break anyway, he thought. He rose from his chair and walked to the water dispenser.

Out of the corner of his eye he saw a figure in the distance. Not again! How many times did they have to check? He stood and drank, enjoying the coolness in his throat, trying to appear unsociable. He looked down at a communal table and pretended to read the free magazine placed there.

Hurry up and pass! he thought. He didn't want any company, just a peaceful drink between an intense few working hours.

As he looked at the magazine, the pages blew over gently. His name was called in a faint whisper.

'Robert.'

Expecting the security guard to be standing next to him, he turned to tell them to stop messing about. No one was there!

He thought the man was maybe playing a childish game. Robert looked everywhere, acting calm. In reality, his hair was standing on end and the adrenaline was pumping through his veins.

OK, I'll just pretend I didn't hear or see anything. Just walk to the desk and carry on as if nothing happened. If it is him messing about, at least I won't look a fool. Just walk to the desk.

Suddenly there was a loud thump that sounded as if it came from the water dispenser he had just left. His head turned so fast it was as if he had been given a hook-punch to the jaw.

Still, no one was in the area.

I'll just call the security desk, he thought, *I wanna know for sure.*

He picked his phone up and dialled an internal number.

'Hello, security desk,' the deep voice answered.

Robert's eyes were scanning the room as he spoke. 'Er, hi. Sorry to bother you. I just wanted to ask if you could check out the floor I'm on. It's just that there was a banging noise a second ago…'

The security guard's voice held a note of disappointment, as if he was being accused of not being up to his job. 'Well, what kind of bang was it, sir?'

Robert wondered why he had to answer such a stupid

question. 'Well, it was like a thump, I guess. I just wanna be sure the place is safe. I haven't really got time to play with, you know what I mean?'

The guard looked at his work colleague and gave some finger gestures to suggest stupidity.

'OK, sir. I'll come and check your floor over myself. According to my colleague you're the only worker in the building. You're on the, er, third floor, right?'

'Yeah. I'd really appreciate that. Sorry to be a pain but I can't really afford any disruptions.'

The guard rolled his eyes but still managed to reply professionally. 'OK, sir, I shall come right up and ease your mind. Maybe we could turn some extra lighting on.'

Robert felt the guard was patronising him now. He replied briefly and ended the conversation.

It's their goddam job anyway! he thought, as he cursed quietly.

One short minute later, a tall, well-built man with an obvious tan came clumsily through the main entrance of the third floor. He reached for some switches, which instantly illuminated the entire floor space. Robert felt a tremendous sense of relief. He hadn't realised the lights were as dim as they were until now.

Initially, the guard did not acknowledge Robert and checked all corners of the floor. He then came over to ask where the noise had come from.

'It was from the water machine, just over there,' Robert explained. 'I thought it was your work colleague checking the area.'

The large man looked a little puzzled. 'We've been on a break for the last hour. Maybe it's just things cooling down – the plastic container I mean. There's no one else in the building and we've checked the entire building over several times already. In fact, we've checked the place out more than we normally do. We've still got another nine or so hours of our shift to go. I guess that shows how bored we get, huh?'

Robert noticed the more relaxed manner of the guard. What had happened to the 'sir?'

He grinned to himself, then replied to the security officer. 'Well, maybe I'm just ultrasensitive to noises tonight. It's so quiet without the daytime air conditioning and the usual chattering. Ignore me: I must be going mad. Thanks muchly for your help. I hope your shift goes quickly for you.'

Robert hoped that that would close the subject and end the conversation that had stalled him from his work, without sounding rude.

'OK, sir. Well, I hope your work goes all right too. You know where I am if you need me.'

I must've been rude, he thought, *the 'sir' thing has returned*!

The guard walked away, left the floor area and decided to leave all of the lights on.

Robert returned to his work, although he couldn't help feeling a little distracted by what had just happened.

Chapter Eight

Chris Milius had his head buried deep in the engine of his car, or so it seemed as Rose came walking towards him. She considered giving him a mischievous fright, but then thought that maybe he would bang his head on the hood. That could lower the mood for the rest of her visit.

'Well, hi there, chickadee,' she said with a fake Texan accent.

He turned and grabbed her around the waist with his fore-arms. He didn't want to stain Rose's lovely white skirt with oil and grease. She appreciated his thoughtfulness and kissed him lovingly on the lips. This developed into a long smooch, as though they had not seen each other for several months.

He backed his head away. 'So, how come you're not at work right now?'

Rose worked as a checkout girl in a large supermarket.

Chris and Rose had been together since the final year of their education. They had grown up together and shared the same school. Rose was content with the simple job and had dreams of a future family.

Chris was now a self-employed mechanic and earned an ample living. At the shared age of twenty-one, the two families and surrounding friends were just waiting for the humble couple to wed.

Rose looked Chris in the eyes seductively. 'I escaped work early for my 'ickle sex piece!'

Chris grinned and weakened at the knees. 'You won't get into trouble, will you?'

She shook her head. 'Are you almost done with work too?' she asked, as she moved her hand up his thigh.

'I can call it a day if that's what you want. I'll lose money for your sexy bod.'

Rose had a well-curved figure, wavy blonde hair and a perfect smile. Chris always felt that she was too good for him. He knew that he was the tall, lanky type. His teeth were ruined by lack of care and his hair was long and straggly. He had never wanted to be in the pretty-boy breed, but his self-esteem was poor.

A sudden ringtone interrupted the start of their personal moment.

Holding Rose with one arm, he took his mobile phone from his back pocket to check the caller's name.

'Who is it, sexy boom-boom?' asked Rose.

'I'm gonna have to take this one, my darling. Just hang about here; it's an important client.' There was a very serious tone to his voice now.

Rose grinned, then placed a well-manicured finger to her mouth. She seductively sucked and licked her finger to show Chris the attention she would soon be giving him.

He walked away and answered his phone, looking a little sheepish.

The phone call was brief, but left Chris with a bead of sweat across his forehead.

'What's the worry, bumpkin?' Rose had noticed his change of mood.

As he returned the phone to a tight pocket, he held her again. 'Just a top client. He'll be coughing up a lot of money soon, so I have to play it cool. Understand?'

Rose nodded, but frowned in suspicion.

He hugged her tightly and told her he was glad she'd come to visit.

Chapter Nine

It was the weekend and all had run fairly smoothly for the week just passed. Relief had set in, as Robert had managed to be ahead of schedule with his work.

'So, since we have the entire weekend thanks to my genius brain – how bout we take a ride out somewhere?' he asked Claire as they both began to wake from a good night's sleep.

Claire was hugging him, her eyes adjusting to the light. 'Sounds good. What did you have in mind?'

'How about a trip to the beach? We can have a good meal and some sun, sea 'n' sand.'

'Well, sounds good if you're paying,' she chuckled.

He moved to hover above her and tickled her vigorously.

'I-I'll pay, you little bugger!' Claire laughed uncontrollably as his strength pinned her down. He continued until she tired from wriggling.

'Come on then!' He bounced up and dressed in less than a minute.

'I'll need a bit more time than that! Us women need to be sure our bodies are ready for display.'

He jumped on her again. 'Oh yeah? I've seen it for the last few minutes and it looks great. So get your arse up. It's already ten o'clock. We could be there for lunch if you're quick.'

She looked worried, 'Rob, I don't wanna put a damper on it, but could we be back for about seven? Only I promised Maria I'd get a couple of drinks with her.'

Robert couldn't hide his slight disappointment. 'OK, I guess we'll still have all day. How come you didn't mention this before?'

'We haven't exactly had much time to talk, have we?'

He looked more forgiving now. 'You're right. We haven't had time for a proper conversation this week.'

He stood and energetically jumped from the bed to the ground.

Claire sat and grabbed for her dressing gown. Once covered, she walked to the bathroom and closed the door behind her.

Robert felt a new tension rise. He sighed quietly as he wondered how they were ever going to have a tension-free day.

The couple managed to get into the car only a few minutes later. Once driving, Robert noticed the roads were comfortably free-flowing, considering it was the weekend. The day was hot with few clouds around.

The day went well. The two swam, sunbathed, ate and laughed a lot.

This was what life's all about!

Robert enjoyed his day of freedom.

The car pulled into the driveway. Robert and Claire looked pink from the sun as they walked back up into the house. Thoughts of what would be done while Claire was away in the evening filtered through Robert's mind.

Time flew past as Claire re-dressed and left the house. She was in such a hurry that she only managed a peck on his cheek. The car drew away as Robert stood in trepidation.

Something's going on, he thought *She's just not the same. Why's she so keen to get away? I've hardly seen her this week. Maybe she needs some female company...* His thoughts fought between good and bad.

As the night grew old, Robert's thoughts became more negative. He fell asleep on the sofa in front of the television.

'Shit!' he suddenly shouted as his eyes opened to daylight.

Robert suddenly remembered it was his big fight-day today. He jumped up and ran upstairs to seek Claire. 'Claire? Claire!'

She rolled in her bed with a weak reply. 'Yeah?'

'I didn't hear you come in! I fell asleep on the sofa.'

'Sorry, baby, I didn't want to wake you. I wasn't too late. I got home soon after midnight.'

'Well, that's OK. I appreciate it, as I've just remembered it's the big day and I haven't done much preparation for it!'

'Rob, you've done years of preparation for it! I tell you what, if you win this fight, at least you could say you didn't do much training for it. If, on the other hand, you lose, then you'll know to prepare better next time, huh?'

Claire surprised herself at how she managed to make such sense first thing in the morning.

Robert's body language froze as he wondered what to do first. 'Right, I have four hours to get prepared and to the venue. The place isn't too far away; I reckon I could do it in half an hour. In the meantime, if you could top the petrol up in the car…'

She looked too relaxed for his eyes. 'Baby, please, just relax. Let's start by getting you looking great. Get yourself in that shower. I'll get your wraps, gloves, shorts, sexy robe and stuff in your kit bag; you concentrate on washing and getting dressed. Everything will be just fine. In fact, tell you what: before we leave, I'll give you a nice shoulder massage.'

Robert could already feel himself relaxing. 'Ooh, hun. I'll just shower up then!' As he walked away, he added, 'I need to get there about an hour early, though, to throw some moves around 'n' get all signed in 'n' stuff.'

'Will you stop?' she said as she dressed herself. 'I've done this with you many times before, remember?'

'Yeah, sorry!' he shouted as he walked into the bathroom.

Time had passed and they managed to arrive at the venue in plenty of time.

Robert was ushered to a dressing room, where he was dressed, his fists strapped and boots tied.

Richard ran into the room looking vexed. 'Man, this guy's tough! I hope you're on top form, buddy!'

Robert felt his shoulders tighten slightly. 'Jees! You're supposed to help me out here!'

'Sorry, dude. You all ready to rock 'n' roll? Let's see them fists!' he shouted aggressively, deliberately to work on Robert's mind. 'You're thinking like a fairy! Come on, get that tough head on!'

Claire stood outside the room listening to the pounding of pads and the boisterous shouting. Her expression told a story of its own. She never really understood Robert's obsession with the sport.

It seemed only a few minutes later that the two men came through the hallway towards the doors that led to the crowds. Robert always looked possessed once his fighting head switched on. The sweat on his face looked as if he'd already fought ten rounds.

Claire reluctantly joined the crowd and sat towards the back. The introductions were made to the crowd and the fight had already begun.

Inside the ring, Robert felt numb. It comforted him slightly to know that Richard stood in his corner.

Their coach was at the older age of sixty-nine. He still had the mental and verbal energy to keep his students working hard. He didn't do much work with Richard and Robert now, but always supported their fights. He stood with Richard to help with the verbal work.

Robert's opponent, Mason, was monstrous. The tall figure had no attractive features. The black mouth guard made him appear even less human.

Let's hope it's a case of not judging by appearances! thought Robert.

Robert felt determined and was the first to move forward with his attack once the bell sounded.

The first round was messy with little control and no distinct rhythm. Punches occasionally clipped chins and ribs, but no distinct hits were made.

The second round came. Mason looked as if he'd switched modes. His punches sunk in deep, hitting Robert hard in the ribs. At one point, Robert felt as if he needed to fall to the ground if he planned on getting any air back into his lungs. Luckily, Mason swung a right hook-punch towards Robert's chin, giving him chance to duck and bring an uppercut back up to knock Mason back briefly. As he felt the connection, it helped Robert's confidence to grow again. In the flow of his opponent moving back with the blow, Robert moved in and threw some jabs and hard punches into the large chin.

Mason dropped back into the ropes and fell to a sitting position. Robert could hear the muffle of crowd cheers as he took the opportunity to get his breath back and loosen his arms and shoulders. He remained focused on his challenge; there was still a lot of work to do.

Mason stood and looked determined to come in for the kill. Robert couldn't help but hold a bit of fear, as he sensed the anger from the monster's humiliation.

Shit! he couldn't help but think.

The monster came ploughing forward again, punching into Robert's ribs. He tried to move away and dig the elbows in tight for protection, but he couldn't escape the large thumps.

He likes my friggin ribs!

In Mason's brief pause, Robert went forward with some more chin jab and punches. A powerful hook-punch knocked his opponent to the side. He lost his bearings briefly and stumbled back in to find Robert. Trying to remain focused and loose, Robert dodged a few punches and kept his distance to avoid the rib smashing.

Round three came. The two were already stumbling with tiredness. Robert was usually the one with amazing stamina. The lack of training was showing!

Mason was the powerful boxer, the type that put too much energy into it too soon. He wouldn't be able to keep it going for long. Robert would have to be fast on his feet, as it'd be hard to stand if the facial punches connected. His coach shouted advice to remind him of this. He stood in the corner, hoping the words were entering Robert's head.

A huge punch came from nowhere, knocking Robert backwards. Another two or three came before he felt himself hit the ground. Pain had left his body and darkness had hit his mind. *Am I dead*? he thought, as he appeared to enter a dream state. A figure stood above him. *Just the ref*, he thought.

At first this was a shadow, but as the figure came closer to Robert's, the familiar face calmed him. 'Dad?' he asked, confused.

'Yes, son. You're at my level of consciousness, but only for a short while. I needed this to happen to give you a very important message.'

Robert was confused. A brief, but clear message was whispered into Robert's ear. His father's figure pulled away now. 'Son, you know what to do. Don't waste time, as time is life.' The figure walked away.

Robert called out but had no response. 'Dad? Dad!' He could now hear the crowd calling mixed messages.

'Get up!' said one. 'Jees, man. Quick!' said another. The second voice he recognised. His eyes blurred and at the same time he noticed his heavy breathing. '...five... six...' He suddenly realised he had time to get up and carry on with the fight. Robert bounced up and held his fists in the ready position. The referee looked into his eyes and moved a finger across them.

'He's fine!' a familiar voice shouted from the corner. *Thanks, Rich.*

The referee hesitated as Robert bounced about to convince everyone he was OK to carry on. Luckily, the ref agreed. Both boxers moved about a bit. Robert felt strangely energised. The bell suddenly sounded for the end of the round.

As Robert sat in his corner, Richard and their coach shouted all sorts of advice at him. None of this seemed to enter his mind. He knew he would win the fight; he had no doubt. His confidence was unusual, especially considering the sight of his opponent.

As he sat with sponges, water and face inspections, he remained focused and ready to bounce back to the fight.

The bell sounded. The two men met roughly central with almost equal confidence. Punches flew from both fighters, with ducks and weaves well timed.

A couple of punches crunched into Robert's ribs again, but the pain was bearable. Robert caught a fist on Mason's jaw. This opened him up to another, then another. Robert's punches were connecting well. His speed increased as he noticed his opponent attempting to duck. The crowd went wild.

Jees, this guy's taking a beating! Tough little bugger! Robert thought. Robert couldn't lose this opportunity to knock his huge opponent down. His speed was an advantage and the gap was there.

'That's it! That's it! Keep going! Come on!' he heard his chum shout from a distance.

His punches were still landing in, thick and fast, as Mason's face became very red, with minor cuts appearing. Robert couldn't help but feel slightly sorry for him, but knew any opponent would do the same, given the opportunity.

Mason was still standing, not having the option of avoidance. He gradually moved closer to the ropes.

One final hook came through, taking him off his balance, spinning him to face away, with both arms dangling over the ropes. Robert moved in close, feeling his aggression build for more.

The referee now intervened. It became obvious that Mason could not continue when he almost hung from his armpits, looking dazed and physically limp.

Robert now stepped back, wondering how he'd become this aggressive person. It won him his fight, but this time it didn't feel like a great thing.

The crowd cheered continuously as Robert walked slowly to his corner, occasionally peering back towards his opponent.

'What's wrong with you? You've won! You've won!' Richard looked amazingly cheerful.

Robert looked back to see Mason's corner men carry him away.

'Don't care about him!' said Richard. 'I wonder how many of your ribs he's bruised 'n' cracked!'

Robert heard the words of his friend, realising he was right.

The announcements were soon made, proclaiming Robert as the winner. The crowd enjoyed the moment and Robert absorbed the feeling of achievement.

The ride home was painful. Robert's ribs were bruised and the adrenaline had worn off. Claire found the silence unbearable. Suddenly he spoke.

'That was my last fight. I'm gonna train, but that was definitely my last fight.'

Claire knew he meant it but couldn't understand what had provoked this decision.

He continued as if he was talking to himself in a mirror. 'I normally see fun in knocking opponents about and proving myself to others, but that's the thing. It's all about image and showing people what I can do. It's like… look at me: I'm a great hero, punching the living daylights out of another human being!'

'They're trying to do the same to you, though,' said Claire. 'It's a competition sport. At least you're using your talents before you grow older and lose them. Many people just sail through life wasting theirs. When you have grandkids at least you can tell amazing stories and give them incentive to do something with their talents.'

'You're right in some ways; it's just starting to seem pointless to me. It's like I'm suddenly becoming this other person.'

'You do seem different, hun. Why think that way now, though? You've fought for so many years and felt good about it. You've come so far. Winning this fight is going to give you options.'

'Yeah. I'm getting closer to pro, but I guess it's just too late now. A couple of years earlier and maybe…'

'Well. I do hate seeing you get hurt, I must admit. Then, of course, there's the moaning for the week or two after the event.'

'I don't moan! It's self-inflicted really, so I do my best not to moan. It's like getting really drunk, then moaning the next day with the hangover.'

'It's not a direct moan: it's like a grumble and the ooh-aah's. It may as well be a proper moan.'

'I never really thought about it, I guess. You usually moan about my moans. Maybe it's time to quit just for that reason. It's probably affecting our relationship without our even realising it.'

'Don't get dramatic; it's quite trivial really. I don't want you to give up something you love. My advice would be that you think about it. You might be going through a phase. Take a break maybe, to see if you miss it. That should tell you all.'

She's right, he thought.

'You're probably right. I don't know what I'm thinking. It seems to be connected to the time I was knocked out. It was very strange. Something weird happened. I saw my dad in like a vision or something. I was knocked out, so don't know if you can dream when you're knocked out. He told me something, but I can't for the life of me remember what he said. I can recall some of his last words, something about not having much time. Maybe I should go 'n' see one of those people; you know the ones.'

'What? You mean a medium?'

'That's it. Where can I find someone like that?'

'Hun, you were knocked out. I'm sure it was just your brain going a bit funny temporarily!'

Robert felt a bit silly now. He looked down with a one-sided grin, wondering why he was thinking so oddly today.

Claire pulled into the drive and they both walked slowly into the house with a couple of sports bags.

Chapter Ten

A couple of days had passed. Robert had recovered well from the fight and had worked late as planned from the start of Monday. It was midweek now and thoughts of the weekend had already begun to enter his head. Sitting at his workstation, Robert dreamt of a sunny weekend involving a good walk to get some fresh air into his lungs. *God, I miss Jack!* he thought. *I must visit him.*

Most Saturdays consisted of a bit of shopping, some visiting of friends, gym training and maybe a bit of television or a film. Sunday was a time to visit Robert's mum, unless there was an organised fight. He sat and thought on how his mum would react to his thoughts on quitting the fighting lifestyle. Would she be glad of it, or would it upset her that he'd no longer be in the local paper?

The computer screen in front of him went into the screen saver mode, making him notice his lack of concentration on his work. 'Shit.'

Another worker close by turned to confirm his ears had heard correctly.

'Sorry, mate. Just a little frustration.'

Robert clicked into work thoughts and continued to key instructions into his computer.

An hour later, he took himself for a walk to the local shop for a pick-me-up. He spotted an energy drink and paid for it.

What were the words Dad whispered? he thought, *I'm sure they were important.*

He continued to walk, thinking about several things. He thought about taking Jack out for a walk to relax his mind.

He pulled his mobile phone from his jacket pocket and found the number he wished to call. Holding the phone to his ear, he squinted to see the view in front of him.

'Hi, Rich? I was just wondering if you'd mind me taking Jack out for a walk this eve? I'm meant to be working late. I'll be coming back to work, but just fancy a break. It'd be nice to see him again.'

What seemed only a few minutes later, Robert and Jack were running together through a local park.

Robert felt as if he'd returned to nature as he ran and rolled in the grass with his old friend.

What on earth did you do to him, Claire? he thought. *This cute thing wouldn't hurt a fly.*

He continued to wonder as they both strolled back towards Richard's home.

Robert reluctantly returned Jack. Richard felt his friend's emotions. 'Take him out as much as you like, buddy. It saves me doin' it.'

Robert knew his friend was only making the offer to cheer him up. Richard and Jack had already bonded quite well.

'Na. I can't confuse him too much. As much as I'd like to take him out everyday, it's probably best that I only do it once every now and then. He's gotta grow up with the owner. I want him to be loyal to you. I can be his part-time pal.'

Richard looked sad. 'What did Claire do to him, man? He seems to like everyone, even the neighbour's cat.'

'Funny you should ask. I don't actually know. She's never been much of an animal-lover, so maybe he senses something. The problem is, it caused so much crap that I daren't bring the subject up again.'

'She's so touchy, your girl. I wish you hadn't married her. I think you could've done so much better, man. You're a top bloke and women scream over you when they see you in the ring. All those women and you chose Claire… she drinks, gets really moody – ya don't want that. You need a fit bird.'

'You've always said that, Rich. It's not about being fit. I like her; she suits me. I find her very attractive. She's going through a strange patch. She'll come out of it.'

'Yeah, well, it's your life. I aint gonna push ya. I'm just being a mate. I just pictured you with the perfect woman. You're the best and you deserve the best.'

Robert punched Richard lightly on the arm. 'Thanks, mate. I

know you're only looking out for me. I really appreciate what you've done for Jack. I know you love him, anyway. I'll watch Claire for a while. I'm sure we'll work through the strange patch. We're getting there. We've had a good few days.'

'Yeah, 'cause you're working too many hours,' Richard joked. He instantly regretted it. There was a pause as the comment passed.

Robert looked at Richard. 'We'll see, OK? Thanks for looking out for me. I'd better get back to work. I don't want any bad stuff going on there!' He turned to walk away.

'Sorry, man. I'll keep my nose out. I'm glad you had a good time with Jack. Come over any time.'

Robert glanced back with a friendly grin as he walked away.

Chapter Eleven

Another couple of late nights of work passed by. Robert worked most of the Saturday to complete his project. A huge feeling of relief filled his body as he realised his goal.

And then it was Sunday.

The Turner couple rose from slumber at a reasonable time. Romance was in the air. A long, passionate kiss was followed by slow lovemaking. Afterwards they hugged in silence, their foreheads touching.

'I should get up,' Robert suddenly whispered.

'Aah. Can't you miss your mother this weekend?' Claire reached down with a provocative hand. 'Can I encourage you to stay?'

Robert smiled and moved closer to her body. 'That's very nice, babe. I must think with my bigger head though. I didn't see her last weekend, so I must make an effort. It'll only be for a couple of hours. We can continue this when I get back if you like.' His hands rubbed over one side of her slender back.

He managed to resist any further contact and slowly rolled out of his side of the bed. Claire's arm went loose and landed on the mattress, her face glum.

'Don't worry! I shall be back as soon as I can. Stay in bed if you like,' he offered.

She managed a smile as he dressed.

He started the car and reversed out of the driveway. A small grin remained on his face as he switched the radio on to hear familiar tunes. He sang along with the catchy songs as he joined a dual carriageway. His speed now increased as he remembered his promise to keep the visit brief.

He skidded slightly as he came off the dual carriageway onto a long country road.

Oops, I'd better slow down.

He came down to a steady speed, taking several sharp bends.

This particular road was always very quiet on a Sunday. He loved the site of the country on either side of the road. The land appeared to go on for ever, up onto grassy hills.

The sun shone, the music was uplifting and Robert's mood was great.

Another bend came; he took it perfectly as he sang pleasantly to the tune. 'I never had a day without you.' The words were thrown to Claire in his own mind.

What's happening to me? It's amazing what sex can do to a man's mind!

A small rabbit ran in front of the car. He swerved perfectly to miss it.

'Nothing can stop me today, ha-ha!' he shouted confidently between the song's lyrics.

He braked hard as a slow moving tractor came into view.

Peering through the side to see the road ahead, he searched for a safe time to overtake.

He found a good time to go, so picked up speed. The tractor suddenly appeared still as he passed it in no time. Another bend came.

Shit! was all he had time to think as a large truck came from a non-existent side road.

Robert slammed his brakes on, hoping his reactions were quick enough to save damage.

A crush of metal was the last thing Robert heard before everything went black.

It was getting late and Claire's concern for Robert's whereabouts was now increasing. She was beginning to come to terms with having to call his mother. Suddenly there was a knock on the door. Claire hoped it would be Robert – maybe he'd forgotten his key.

On opening the door, she recognised the woman despite her difference in presentation. This time she stood in jeans and T-shirt with her hair down.

'You were here to take Jack away before, weren't you?' she asked. 'The one they carted away in the ambulance.'

'Yeah, that's me. My name is Sally,' she nervously replied.

'Well, are you better now? What actually happened?' Claire was trying to work out the reason for her casual visit.

'I'm fine. In fact, that's what I've come here to talk about. I'm not here to see Jack.'

'Oh, Jack's not here now. We decided it'd be best if he went to another home. I was a little harsh before. Robert, my husband, sorted my head out in the end.' She looked down in guilt.

'That's good. Is he settled in his new home, do you know?' Sally's eyes looked bright and pleased.

'Yeah. It's Rob's friend who has him now. He loves dogs too. He was actually looking to get a dog soon anyway.' There came a long, uncomfortable pause.

'Sorry, Sally. Do you wanna come in for a drink?'

'That'd be good. I feel I need to tell you something. You can tell me to shove off if you want,' Sally said nervously as she followed Claire through the hallway to the kitchen.

'Why would I do that? I'm just waiting around for Rob to come back. You could take my mind off him for the minute.'

'I guess you must think I'm weird, coming over after the last event.'

'Na. Everyone gets sick. It's just when and where that can be embarrassing. The human body strikes back at the most awkward times!'

'Well, there's a little more to what happened, but I think we should settle with our drinks before I explain.'

Claire glanced at Sally oddly as she switched the kettle on and reached for two cups.

The two ladies settled in the living room. They sat opposite each other, one on each sofa. Sally thought it'd be best that way, in preparation for a bad response.

'Well… I'm sitting in anticipation!' said Claire. 'What've you got on your mind?'

The pressure was on. Sally took a sip of tea.

'OK, this is hard to approach, but when I came close to Jack and prepared the injection, a strange thing happened.'

'Yeah?' Claire prompted.

'Err… as I reached to begin the process, I was pushed.'

'By that man? I hope you sorted him out!'

'No. Phil is a great guy. He wouldn't hurt a soul. He hates putting animals down, even if they're severely ill.'

'So you're not talking about a physical push, then? Maybe a psychological one... a push to get the ball rolling with the putting-down of Jack?' Claire needed a rational explanation.

'This is where you may ask me to leave.' Sally looked down at her drink.

'Come on, Sally! Spit it out! My husband is out longer than he said he'd be and I'm starting to get worried. No offence, but it'd be good if we could shift this along so that I can start thinking about making some calls.'

Claire was beginning to think this was becoming a nuisance and it certainly wasn't helping her at this moment in time.

'I'm sorry. Maybe I should come back another time. It's a rather sensitive matter.'

'Is this related to my husband?'

'No. Please, just hear me out; then I'll go.'

There was another uncomfortable moment of silence.

'OK,' Sally began again. 'I said I was pushed, right? Well, I... I think I was pushed by something that wasn't alive.'

Claire was even more confused now and frowned as she sipped her drink.

'You see, Phil was comforting Jack and I was the one who was about to administer the injection. Some presence pushed me back. It was, maybe... a ghost.' Her last words were almost whispered.

'A ghost?' Claire answered sarcastically.

Sally looked very uncomfortable but was determined to give her story.

Claire stirred and moved her head forward. Her eyes glared at the nervous lady. 'Look, I am waiting and worried for my husband and you're telling me that the last time you came to my house you were pushed by a ghost? Did you get treated with a few drugs when you were carted away in that ambulance?'

Sally put her drink on the floor. 'I knew this was a stupid idea.'

'Damn right it was a stupid idea!' Claire found herself steaming with anger.

Sally stood immediately and walked to the front door.

Claire watched. 'That's it,' she said, a little calmer. 'You run off now. I think I may just make a call to report you escaping that home you're meant to be detained in!'

Sally shifted quickly through the front door as it slammed behind her.

'Stupid cow! What the hell was that all about? Bloody wasting my time like that!' Claire said to herself as she walked towards the telephone.

She dialled a number.

'Hello?' Claire asked cautiously, then paused.

'I'm sorry to bother you, Mrs Turner, but I was just concerned about Rob. Is he still with you? Only he hasn't come home yet and he's not normally this long. I mean, if he is still there, that's OK, but he said he'd be back in a couple of hours. He normally does as he says.'

Claire allowed time for the lady to respond to the question. The answer left Claire drained of colour.

'Oh. I'm sure he just popped over to Richard's or something. I'll catch him on his mobile. No need to worry. He can look after himself,' she convinced Robert's mum.

There was a brief silence from both women.

'OK, well, I'd better get going. Sorry to have disturbed you… thank you… bye now… bye.' She lowered the handset to its stand.

She picked up a small phone book from a side table and found Robert's mobile phone number. Dialling it she held her breath in hope.

A short moment later she had a recorded message come through. 'The phone you are calling is switched off. Please try again later.'

Dialling it, she held her breath. Claire's expression changed to a strange mix of panic and something you couldn't quite put your finger on…

She thought she would give it just a little longer – an hour maybe – before calling the police.

Chapter Twelve

Chris Milius sat in his car. The driver's seat was almost horizontal as he relaxed with a cigarette. The window was slightly open but not helping to clear the mass of smoke. The car was filled with a haze.

It was dark outside, but extra so where the car sat on the side of a quiet road. There were no streetlights, only the moon and the stars to gaze at.

A sudden knock at the passenger window made him sit bolt upright in fright. In recognition of the visitor, he reached across to open the door.

'Why do you have to stink the car out like that? I wasn't that long,' the girl whispered, as if sneaking into an assembly at school.

'Sorry, sexy. I was just chillin' out. Are you ready to go?'

'Yeah. How long will this take anyway?'

He looked at her, concerned. 'Ah, I just have to pop in and out. After that we can drive south to the Eurotunnel. We'll be the rich gypsies we've always wanted to be!'

'Mmm… travelling. No more stupid working with stupid people, with a stupid wage,' she said aggressively, throwing her hands in the air.

'I thought you didn't mind that job, Rose.'

'I had to work. Why do we do things we have to do rather than what we want to do? Everyone's always telling me that life's too short and that we shouldn't do the things we dislike.'

'Well, I guess we're too young to know what we want to do. Some people love their jobs. Once I pick this money up, we'll be able to do what we want to do. So don't worry, sexy. You should be happy right now. Come on.' He reached and pulled her head towards him, to encourage one of their romantic moments.

They kissed for a while.

He was the first to pull back. 'Come on then, you! Let's go get our package!'

He reached to pull his chair seat up to an acceptable angle for driving and turned the ignition key.

He pulled out into the lane. He drove for twenty minutes before heading into a residential area. Driving into a dead-end road, he pulled into a wide driveway. He pulled up and put on the handbrake.

'Right. I won't be long. You stay right where you are and keep the locks down until I actually reach for the door handle. Understand?'

'Yeah. What are you expecting to happen, then? I thought you were just picking up a cheque.'

His eyes darted to the house. 'Nothing's gonna happen. You should always lock a car up when you're just sitting in it. Especially at night. I don't want anyone pinchin' my sexy baby, now do I?'

She smiled more comfortably now. 'OK, well, don't be long, just as you promised.'

He looked at her with a knowing smile as he opened the car door to step out.

She watched while locking the car doors.

He stood at the front door of the house and knocked as if he'd entered a code into the wood. The door opened slightly. Chris said something, which in turn allowed him access. The person behind the door stepped backwards into the shadows as he opened it.

Suddenly, a figure was pushed out of the front door, tripping over their feet as they fell backwards.

A sudden *bang*, followed by an almost instant shot of light, jerked the figure that had fallen.

Rose's adrenaline pumped around her body, making her freeze in fright.

'Chris?' she whispered, noticing the shape of her partner on the floor.

As she looked up, she caught sight of a figure holding a gun in the doorway. In a panic, she ducked below the height of the dashboard, breathing heavily.

Thoughts of escape ran through her head. The biggest problem in her mind was the visualisation of crawling to the driver's seat. She instantly wondered if the keys had been left in the ignition.

Sweating and breathing heavily, she pondered over the thought of looking up in order to work out the next move.

As if it was too painful to move, Rose lifted her head to eye level with the lowest part of the windscreen. As her eyes adjusted, she noticed that the darkness in front of her was actually the figure from the doorway, hovering over the window.

A shocked whimper came from her mouth as the windscreen shattered from the force of a large tool.

Her instincts told her to run rather than attempt to drive. It may've been too late after an attempted climb over the seats. She opened the passenger door and began to flee.

As she ran, a shot rang out and something landed in her right thigh. She felt the deep pain immobilise her leg.

As she fell, the stranger walked over to her, as if he was taking a casual stroll. He stood over her and paused. A strong, deep, slow-paced voice sounded.

'He screwed up. I gave him a simple task and he screwed up.'

Rose lay in pain and shock, breathing heavily, trying to move her injured leg. Nothing mattered now.

She knew she was about to die. 'Who the... hell are you?' she managed to ask, her words breaking.

The man laughed. The sound was chilling. 'He kept it quiet, then, hoping you'd think he'd done a huge job. Innocent cash. Yeah... well, now I have to finish a job he couldn't do. If you want something doing, do it yourself.'

Rose tried to move again in one last hope, but the pain was paralysing. She began to cry. At first the noise was faint, changing to a loud cry of dread.

The stranger stood in silence, as if a stroke of sympathy had overshadowed his cruelty.

Suddenly, his hand rose slightly. The final shot was heard, as the young woman's head hit the ground.

Chapter Thirteen

Claire sat in the hospital waiting room.

A nurse passed several times without acknowledging the distressed people on the plastic chairs. Claire sat leaning forward with her hands clamped together.

'Mrs Turner?' a strong female voice called from the distance.

Claire looked to find the voice and spotted a large lady walking towards her.

She stood. 'Yes.'

'He's a lucky man. Thankfully the airbag and seat belt did a good job. Don't get too excited though. He's concussed and has a few cuts and bruises. He does look a bit of a mess.'

'Can I see him, then?' Claire asked in frustration.

'Follow me. The nurse is just finishing off.'

They both walked down a long, white corridor and turned right into a private room.

Robert managed a smile as Claire came into view. His head was cut and swathed in bandages. Claire tried to assess the damage.

She moved towards his bedside and touched his cheek.

'Come here,' he said, as he grabbed her with his uninjured hand and kissed her lovingly on the lips.

She moved back slightly. 'They said you hit a lorry at quite a speed!'

'Hey, with the punches I've taken in my life time, you think a lorry's gonna finish me off?'

Claire grinned in surprise. 'I was just expecting worse…'

'Na! It's not my time yet. I'm too young. They say once the concussion clears I can go home.'

She held his hand in silence as the nurse tidied her tray at the opposite side of the room.

Robert broke the quiet moment. 'They said the lorry had no driver, but that they have fingerprints to go by on the steering wheel. Don't you think that's a little odd?'

'The lorry had no driver?' Claire frowned in confusion.

'Well, they seem to think it was either a prankster or some deliberate act from some punk.'

'So, someone started the truck up, drove it to the middle of the lane, then jumped out?'

'That's how it seems.' He raised his eyebrows.

Claire narrowed her eyes in thought.

'I mean, why would someone attempt to kill the odd driver on the road for some prank? The world's gone crazy!' He was now frowning in anger.

Claire moved backwards.

'You OK, honey?'

'I just think this whole thing's idiotic! I hope they find the driver. If they do, I'd like to question him myself! I take it the car's a write-off?'

'Yep. The lorry was smashed up at the side and the driver behind me was so slow driving anyway that he stopped in good time.'

'So you were doing your speeding thing again?'

Robert realised he'd said the wrong thing. Claire was now facing him with a fierce expression. He was taken back to his childhood: mother telling him off.

'I was doing a steady speed. I overtook the slow guy, as he seemed to be doing five miles per hour. The speed limit was fifty. I was still under that.' He tried to dig himself out from the psychological hole.

'Mmm. The police know that too, do they?'

'Well, I guess so… honey, I haven't done anything wrong. This idiot tried to kill me!' He needed her sympathy more than ever.

During that moment, a familiar figure walked into the room. 'Robert!'

His mother ran over and hugged Robert tightly. Her eyes were brimming with tears.

Claire suddenly felt inferior and decided to walk into the corridor. Robert noticed her discomfort and accepted her evasion.

'Hi, Mum. It's OK.' He winced as her hug hurt some of the bruising.

'Claire freaked me out when she basically said you should've been at mine. I guessed something awful must've happened when neither of you answered your phones. Why didn't anybody tell me?'

Her eyes were even more tearful as she felt the pain of not being informed.

'Mum, we would've told you. It's literally only just settled down. The nurse has just this second finished off cleaning and bandaging me up,' he managed to explain, as he felt the effects of the drugs kick in.

'OK, my boy. That's OK, then. You look as if you want to sleep some of this off now. Shall I come back later?' She suddenly appeared one hundred percent relaxed.

'It's suddenly hit me, Mum. I'm getting a little drowsy.'

She kissed him on the forehead. 'I shall come and see you tomorrow. Get your rest now. I'll tell Claire I'm leaving.'

She walked away gracefully. Robert had hoped to have seen Claire for another minute before he fell sleep, but his eyes grew heavy.

Robert noticed a police officer look in his direction from just outside the ward door. A nurse approached him and said a few words. The scene blurred as he fell into a deep sleep.

Chapter Fourteen

Richard, Rachael, Robert and Claire were sat in the front room of the Turners' house. Robert had one small plaster remaining on his forehead. He sat comfortably on the floor in front of Claire, as the others spread over the sofas. The television flickered in the background as everyone held a mug of coffee. A small table in the middle of the room held crisps and small sausage rolls.

'All I wanna say is welcome home, buddy. I'm so glad it wasn't serious shit, man.'

Robert grinned as his friend attempted to show a bit of heart.

Claire looked at Robert. 'It certainly was a close one! It just makes ya realise a few things, especially that us humans are more fragile than we think,' she said as she stroked Robert's hair.

'Argh. You guys know I aint human. I gave that truck a good kicking!'

Everyone laughed politely.

Richard leant forward. 'So, did you hear anything from the police? It makes me so angry that these idiots get away with murder!'

Robert began to show annoyance. 'They say they've matched the prints up with some guy. Apparently him and his girlfriend have both gone missing. They're trying to get information from parents and friends.'

Rachael spoke for the first time. 'That sounds odd. That doesn't make sense at all.'

Everyone sat in silence for what seemed like a couple of minutes.

'Well, I guess it's more important that our friend's still alive 'n' kickin',' said Richard at last.

Everyone agreed. It went quiet again as they all glanced at the television.

'A lot of weird stuff is happening lately. I just want everything to return to normal now. Work's gonna be annoyed now, though, as I'm behind schedule.'

Robert looked at his right hand, wondering if it'd be ready for some heavy typing.

'Stuff work, man!' said Richard. 'Health comes first! They'll understand. You've always worked hard for them. They can't expect anything else after what you've been through. Make sure you take the whole time off! You've got another week, aint ya?'

'Yeah. I'm pretty much healed up though, so I'm gonna be bored if I can't do very much.'

Richard looked mischievous. 'Why don't you ease back into training at the gym? It always aids recovery.'

Claire looked horrified. 'No way! You've been told to take things easy and that's what I'm going to make sure you do.'

Rachael agreed with a knowing nod.

'Ah. Well, it's not a bad idea! I have virtually no bruising left, just a couple of remaining cut marks. I'm ready to do some exercise. It always speeds the healing process up for me anyway.' Robert tried to sound convincing.

'I'm not taking the blame for anything you mess up, then!' She folded her arms in protest.

Robert grinned and patted Claire on the back of her neck in jest.

She unfolded her arms as she remembered something. 'I forgot about this thing by the way, what with everything going on… that vet woman who came to the house before, appeared at the door on the day of your accident…' She looked at Robert for a reaction.

'Yeah? Did she come to ask about Jack?'

'No. She told me this strange story about how this ghost had pushed her to the floor when she tried to put Jack down.'

'It got that close?' Robert said in disgust.

'Well, yeah, if it wasn't for the push, it probably would've been done before you came home to check up on me.' Claire realised she'd opened a wound and began to panic over a potential argument.

'*Jees*! I can't believe that.' He looked horrified and angry at the same time.

The room went quiet as the tension grew.

'I'm sorry, I thought you knew. I wouldn't have mentioned it if I'd thought you didn't know.'

The room continued to grow silent as Robert was too disgusted to say anything more on the subject.

Richard attempted to break the tension. 'OK, well, what's done is done, guys. At the end of the day, Jack's still alive and healthy. What was the story on the ghost, though? Me 'n' Rachael are waiting on that bit... come on, Rob! You're holding the fun bit up!'

Robert gave a slightly friendlier expression towards the keen couple. 'I guess I did restrain the fun part of that story.' He reached for Claire's leg and tapped her thigh gently. 'Come on, then; I'll let you finish.' He looked at Rachael and Richard. 'Sorry, guys. I didn't mean to create an issue there.'

Claire felt guilty and didn't really feel like continuing with the story. She made an effort, however, to entertain the guests. 'As I was saying... this vet woman said that when she was about to give Jack the injection, a hand pushed her to the ground. It wasn't a human hand. She said it was from something that wasn't alive.'

Richard laughed. 'A dead hand?'

Claire smiled. 'By that, I'm sure you can understand why I asked her to leave. I told her she must've been drugged up after she had a funny turn.'

'That was a bit harsh. It could be true. A lot of weird things have happened to me lately. I haven't told you though, 'cause I don't wanna be accused of being mad,' Robert said quite seriously.

'What sort of things have you had happen, then?' Rachael asked shyly.

'Well, things have fallen for no reason; bangs have gone off at work with no explanation; I had a vision when I was knocked out briefly during my fight.'

'That sounds coincidental, hun,' Claire responded. 'Bangs and things always go off in buildings. I'm sure there's a rational explanation for them. And you were knocked out, babe. It's not unusual to see strange things when your brain's been hammered.'

Rachael let out a quiet giggle.

'She's right, you know. It's not really much to go on, Rob,' Richard agreed.

'Oh, man! I know in my mind that these things were just a bit too weird to bluff off as normal.' His defence was becoming apparent.

Claire spoke up. 'So you're saying you believe this woman?'

'I'm saying I wouldn't have dismissed the possibility. I'm quite open-minded about these things.'

'Well, if you wanna know more, Rob, her number's on the side of the phone. Just ask for Sally.'

Robert felt her tone of voice lower in disappointment.

Richard helped out again. 'So hang on a minute! What's the vision all about? We dismissed that part!'

'Ah, you don't wanna hear it.' Robert seemed cagey now.

'Yeah, I do. I promise not to make fun.'

There was a moment's silence. 'OK. Well, I can't really remember much about it. All I remember is the thought of my dad stopping to talk to me. The problem is... I can't remember what he said. It seemed very important though. The good thing was that I came round in time to carry on with the fight and felt very invigorated.' He paused. 'The strangest thing was that although my fighting and stamina seemed to improve, I also knew that that would be my last competition fight.'

'What?' Richard looked disgusted. 'There's no way you can give up fighting now! You've come so far. That fight has taken you to the next league, man!'

'I was just telling you about my vision. It might just be a phase, a temporary way of thinking.'

'It'd better be! I tell you what: if you can have the option of making a huge career of this or just opting out, I'd be very cross if you chose the latter. As a friend, you owe it to me, dude!'

Claire let out a quiet tut and looked in Rachael's direction, hoping she'd have a similar thought.

Unfortunately, Rachael was glaring at the television in ignorance. Claire hoped that that was her way of showing lack of interest in the boxing subject.

Richard turned to Claire. 'You've gotta encourage the boy. So many years of training, finally hits the professional levels... he can't give up now, man.'

Claire just returned a thin grin.

Robert was expecting more than silence from her usual, outspoken ways.

Maybe he's made enough of a point to keep her quiet for a change, he thought.

Richard brought things back to a neutral subject. 'Oh well; the most important thing is that Rob has to get fit again.' He looked at the couple opposite him and raised his mug. 'So here's to health and happiness.'

'Health and happiness,' everyone responded, and the mugs clashed.

Chapter Fifteen

Robert sat bored at home. Crisps sat to the left of him and a couple of books on computer programming to the right. An active news page was viewed on the television.

Claire was at work. He sat wondering how he could get through the week without going crazy. *Jees*, he thought, *This is stupid!*

He looked across at the telephone, just visible in the hallway through the doorway. Getting up, he walked towards the telephone book at its side. He picked it up and walked through the pages with two fingers.

Sally.

He found the name.

Can't hurt. Just a chat. I'm desperate.

'Hello?' A gentle, curious female voice sounded in Robert's ear.

'OK, hello. Er... I'm sorry to bother you. I just wanted to introduce myself and apologise about something. You don't know me, but you met my wife recently.'

'OK.' Another curious-sounding response.

He felt pushed to continue. 'Well, our dog, Jack, kind of pinned her in the corner in our kitchen. After that, she planned to have him put down, but luckily, for me it didn't happen.'

A short pause. 'I'm amazed she didn't insist on it. Not being funny, but she didn't seem the easy-going type... no offence!'

'Er... well, you're right there. Luckily, she gave me a chance to take him to a good home.'

A sigh of relief came over the phone. 'Thank God for that! Only, I see people wanting to put their animals down for such crazy reasons. I mean, if they did that to humans... I mean, just imagine it.'

She seemed to struggle for the right words.

'Yeah. I love Jack, so it was very difficult for me to even think about such a thing. I knew that there was just something Jack didn't like about Claire for some strange reason. It's best just to pass him over to a family or person that he likes.'

There was a slight pause. Sally was first to speak. 'So, what was your name? Did you want me to help you in some way?'

She suddenly sounded very efficient, as if she realised she was actually meant to sound professional.

Robert felt slightly awkward for a couple of seconds. 'Oh, sorry. I meant to get to the point. Er... the name's Robert Turner and, as I say, I'm husband to Claire Turner. She, er, said you spoke to her the other day about a strange occurrence in our home...'

There was a sharp intake of breath at the other end of the phone. Then Sally spoke wearily, as if she'd suddenly become slightly breathless. 'I, er, didn't think your wife was interested.'

Robert felt a small grin appear on his face. 'Well, she's very closed-minded, you know. She won't accept anything other than what she can see with her own eyes.'

'Robert, will you listen to my story, then? You sound a lot calmer than your wife,' she said, laughing nervously.

'Of course I will. She told me some of it. She said you were pushed by a hand...' He tried to encourage the conversation forward.

'Yes! I hope you'll let me explain. You see, I've never experienced anything like this before. My own mother thinks I'm going crazy, but I swear—'

Robert interrupted. 'Trust me, Sally: a lot of strange things have been happening to me lately. It'd be nice to hear someone else's odd goings-on.'

'OK. I shall tell you the whole thing, but only if you promise not to shout, laugh or make fun of me. I'll put the phone down if you react in any of those ways.' Her voice sounded very defensive.

'Sally, come on. We've been OK so far, haven't we? As I say, I've had some strange things happen to me and, to be honest, I'm very curious as to what happened in my home that day.'

Sally's voice calmed. 'OK, Robert. Sorry. It's just that that's all I've had from people so far.'

Robert didn't know what else to say, so hoped that the explanation would come soon.

'Right,' she started. 'Well, when I tried to give Jack his injection, a large, strong hand pushed me back. It wasn't my colleague's hand. His hands were down and too far away. Besides, he's not that kind of person. I've known him for years.' Her words were rushed and nervous.

'OK, Sally. I believe you. Did you get to see the size or shape or anything distinctive about the hand?'

'Well, it was all a blur. I just remember a large, strong hand. It was so fast; I mean, it just pushed me over. It – or he – didn't give me time to see anything, really.'

'Was it larger than the average hand, would you say?'

'Well, yeah. I guess so.'

'Thank you, Sally. I guess I just need to work out what that was all about. So many strange things are happening lately. I'm starting to think that it's some kind of puzzle… or someone or something trying to tell me something. I guess even my saying that is a bit of a puzzle in itself.'

'So, you believe me, then? That's unusual. This isn't some kind of wind-up, is it?'

Robert felt slightly cross that this lady needed a lot of reassurance. He breathed in deeply to calm himself and replied pleasantly.

'Honestly, Sally, I believe you, and I really appreciate you talking to me today about something you find so difficult. If you remember anything else then please let me know, won't you?'

'Yeah, sure. I'm so glad you believe me! You really have made my day just listening to me like this.' The confidence grew in her voice. *Thank God for that*! he thought.

'OK, look, Sally… I'm gonna go now, but I do really appreciate your time and honesty. Thank you very much.'

It was obvious to Robert that Sally was now smiling on the other end of the phone.

'Thank you, Robert. Thank you so much. I will definitely call you if I can remember anything else from the event.'

They both said their goodbyes and placed the phones on the receivers.

Chapter Sixteen

As the week passed, Robert grew more thoughtful about the strange events that had occurred recently in his life. The television was there to entertain, but his thoughts were most definitely on other things.

Claire had been evasive and distant, claiming that she'd worked hard in the daytime. Robert found her behaviour hard to deal with.

She would return home, kiss him on the cheek, then throw her baggage in a corner, only to pick up cleaning materials. Her habits became predictable. Something needed cleaning every day. Robert wasn't sure if she was finding it difficult to deal with the recent events, or finding things to occupy herself in order to avoid his company. Either way, his concern grew as the week moved on.

Thursday came. Robert had slept due to boredom for most of the day. Inspiration for exercise and work had finally enveloped his mind. He rose from his lazy position on the sofa, the woollen blanket falling from his body. He stretched with what felt like great strength.

If I pop to the gym now, he thought, *I'll get at least two hours' training in before Claire comes home. I could surprise her with a prepared meal. Maybe that's what she needs to see – that I'm still there for her.*

He went to the gym and managed a decent training session, leaving him feeling revitalised. A cool shower invigorated him enough to make him feel sharp.

Robert soon arrived home to follow through with his cooking idea. The breakfast table was covered with a pure white cloth and a couple of decorative candles. He'd prepared a large tray of chicken pieces and a variety of vegetables. The food was presented in silver trays, the ones he knew only came out for special guests or large get-togethers.

The table was slightly small and looked smothered in food

delights – barely room for the plates. He sat admiring what he'd achieved in a short space of time.

Maybe seductive clothing as well, he thought.

His idea drove him to a smart shirt and trousers. They sat to the rear of his wardrobe in their bedroom. The shirt was no ordinary shirt to his wife: this one Claire had picked as his 'going-out' shirt in their early years of dating. It always worked on the encouragement of seduction. She said it displayed his figure in a teasing way. Claire had to make Robert promise that he would only ever wear it under her supervision.

As Robert reminisced over those days, he found himself chuckling to himself. His thoughts were suddenly interrupted by the entrance of Claire.

Panicking to accomplish his task, he quickly grabbed the clothing to change into. He could hear rustling downstairs but continued with his determination to impress. The noise downstairs ended. Robert felt as if he could feel her thoughts and grinned to himself as he imagined her expression on first sight of the table. He zipped his trousers and fastened the final button on his outfit.

Claire's voice suddenly boomed through the house, as if she knew his exact location. 'Robert! I'm just out for a bit. I won't be late home though, so I'll probably catch you when I get back!'

His instant thoughts were to grab her quickly before leaving the house. The door slammed as he cried, 'Wait, I—!'

His thoughts seemed to crash at his feet. He wondered whether to chase her or let her go. Either way, slight anger had now entered his body.

She must've smelt the food! She must've looked about! *Damn her!* he thought, as he sat on the bed in disbelief.

He ran downstairs and attempted to call her on the mobile. As he heard a ringtone close by, he realised she'd left her phone behind.

He put the phone down and lifted it again.

I'll probably regret this!

As soon as he dialled the number he spoke in a hurry. 'Rich! Listen, mate. I've got an issue. I don't want your Rachael to overhear. Could you come over to mine quick-quick?'

He gave only a couple of seconds' opportunity for a response, then placed the phone down.

Robert ran upstairs and changed his shirt for a white, sleeveless T-shirt. As he walked away from the bedroom, he caught sight of himself in a mirror. After a short glare, he ruffled his hair aggressively.

I've had enough of this crap!

The sound of Richard's motorbike interrupted Robert's thoughts. He ran clumsily downstairs and opened the front door to a confused face.

'Rob. What the f—'

Robert pushed him towards his bike. 'Please, man. Trust me. I just need a fast ride to town. I don't have the car.'

Richard hesitated, but complied with the request. 'Come on, man. You'd better give me time later for an explanation.'

Richard grabbed another helmet from his bike's compartment and shoved it into Robert's chest.

The bike turned gently, then sped off into the darkness.

The narrow streets suddenly opened to a burst of public houses and nightlife. People were stumbling across the roads, shouting and joking.

Richard pulled into a small parking zone, pushed his bike stand down and climbed off.

Robert was removing the helmet and hurrying to get up.

Richard lifted his visor. 'Rob, you've just recovered from a crazy accident. What kind of trouble are you about to get into? I've only seen you like this once... that was when you went after that punk Jeff. Look where that landed you! A night in the cell – for a pointless fight. All I ask is that you think rationally. OK?'

'Rich, I'll tell you if anything comes of this. I aint gonna do anything crazy; I just need to see if I'm going mad or not.'

Robert's eyes were focused and determined. His body was tense, waiting to pounce.

He looked Richard in the eyes as he asked, 'Could you just hang out here for about half an hour? Please? If I'm not back, then just go home. I'll be OK; I'll just grab a taxi.'

Richard looked towards the happy crowd in the near

distance, then returned a serious look. 'OK, but if you need me to come along and help out, I don't mind. We're old buddies, man. You know how much we look after one another. Let me in, man.'

Robert looked down and sighed. Richard reached to hold his shoulder. 'Let me in, man. Trust me.'

'OK.' Robert whispered. 'I think Claire's having an affair. She's been acting strange all week. Every time I get close she avoids me. Tonight she just went out without an explanation. I'm sure I'm not just imagining it. We haven't been right for a while now. Her eyes, her actions. I just know it.'

'Jees, man. She may just be going through a weird patch. You know how women can be. How d'you know she's out here anyway?' Richard's voice was soft. He folded his arms.

'She took the car. She's been drinking lately, so these were my first thoughts.'

'So you're saying she's been drink-driving these days?'

'I dunno, man. I don't know anything anymore. Can I just check these pubs out? If she aint in any, I'll speak to her in the morning to work out what's going on.'

Richard noticed Robert's muscles relax. 'I'll come with you, then. You can check the couple of pubs on the left; I'll check the three on the right. I promise to be thorough. I think it's crazy, but if it clears your mind a bit, then I'll help you out, man.'

Robert tapped his friend on the arm and began walking towards the small crowd ahead.

Richard watched for a second as he stored his helmets and locked his bike.

It didn't take long to walk through the first pub. The crowds were heavy, but the lighting was good.

Robert bought a small drink from the bar and scanned the entire public area. A confident lady approached him.

Initially he found himself attracted to the long, curly blonde hair. Her face had light make-up, apart from the bright red lipstick, which seemed to be the area she wanted to overstate.

Her lips opened. 'Hi there. Whatcha doin' standin' here all alone? Do you need some company?'

He stood silent as she probed. 'You look like the strong silent type. Very sexy… what are you looking for here?'

He finally placed his glass on the bar and responded. 'Thanks for showing an interest. It has honestly boosted my ego, but I'm actually looking for my wife. She's out tonight and we're meant to meet up at some point.' He gave a gentle grin and walked to the exit ahead. The lady watched and admired.

An argument was breaking out in the street as he passed to the next door. As he entered, the music hit his ears, causing them to ring instantly. The room was dark, with coloured lights moving randomly through the air. He felt people watching his moves as he walked to find the main bar. Once found, he leaned against it, trying to look comfortable.

It was hard to see, so he focused on searching for the right figure. He knew his wife's shape as well as he knew his own.

People were dancing everywhere. There was no designated dance floor. People were knocking chairs over and looking as if they were deliberately trying to trash the place.

Surely she wouldn't be here, he thought.

He'd given up and begun to walk out, when he saw Richard running in.

Richard couldn't see in front of him as he entered. He looked like a worried blind man. Robert ran over and grabbed him by the arms. 'I'm here. There's nothing to see. I'm really sorry… bad judgement on my part!'

'She's out!' Richard shouted in panic. 'She's out with that woman… Maria. The one from work… she's with a woman; it's OK.'

Robert sighed in huge relief. 'Why do you look so panic-stricken then?'

'I think she saw me. They were both chatting to a bloke. I'm assuming they're just chatting and that it's something to do with work. We can't jump to conclusions. I was just worried that you were gonna keep looking and see them in there, then jump to the wrong conclusion. It looks innocent. We need to get you back home though. Quick!'

'So it looks like nothing?' Robert pried.

'It looks like a quick drink after work. It looks OK. I just don't want you getting the wrong idea and ruining everything when it's nothing. You get me?'

Robert frowned slightly, then relaxed.

They both walked fast to the motorbike and rode off.

Chapter Seventeen

The speakers roared with guitar music as Matthew Carter glanced at his watch in a relaxed, seated position. The room was dim, leaving his features in shadow as he waited patiently. He reached for his glass of red wine as he repeatedly checked his wristwatch on his other arm.

The music suddenly stopped and beeping – leading to the hourly news – hit the air.

'This is the three o'clock news… and two bodies have been uncovered in a park in the small village of Weyfall, in Berkshire. Investigators say that bullet wounds were the cause of their deaths. Local police are calling for any witnesses that may have been in the area…'

Matthew hit the power button on the remote control. The speakers silenced instantly.

He finished the glass of red wine and slammed it on the coffee table in front of him.

'Clever bastards!' he shouted. 'This is getting too complicated!'

Time to lie low for a while, he thought.

He picked his mobile phone up and dialled a number. The receiving phone barely rang when it was answered.

His tone of voice had now changed. 'Hi. You're gonna have to be patient with me. Things are pretty busy right now, but I promise things'll be OK. You know how much I need you. I've just got to sort this out carefully.'

He sat there quietly as he allowed a response.

His voice then came through slightly croaky as he said his final words. 'Right. I do love you. You know that, right?' He allowed a brief reply. 'OK then. Bye for now.'

★

DI Raymond sat opposite Robert Turner. The atmosphere was tense.

My last day of relaxation and freedom and I get this shit! Robert thought.

The detective probed with another question. 'So you never knew this Chris Milius?'

'Like I said, I don't know the guy. The information from you is all I have.'

The man's face flushed further. His grey hair appeared even greyer as the colour of his face changed. 'OK, sir. Well, I'd really appreciate if you could run through your traffic accident again.'

Robert looked impatient as he fiddled with a thin marking on the table. The interview was held in his own home. The breakfast-room table seemed smaller than ever with the intense questioning.

Why do I feel like the bad guy? he wondered. *I've done nothing wrong.*

'I've made my report – statement – whatever you call it. Why do I have to run through it again? *What relevance does this have to his death?* Robert thought to himself.

'Please cooperate, sir. I'm just looking for every bit of detail that anyone has on this man, so that we can trace his prior moments. Everything helps.'

'OK,' said Robert more understandingly. 'Well, like I said – I was driving along; I came up behind this really slow tractor. I decided to over take when I thought it was safe – still under the speed limit, I must add. What seemed only a few seconds after, this truck pulls out of a side lane… I brake really hard, but can't avoid hitting the thing.'

'Did you get a glimpse of the person inside?'

'I can't remember seeing the person, just the object I tried to avoid.'

'OK, sir, well…' The detective's words were interrupted by the loud opening of the front door.

'That'll be my wife,' said Robert. 'She can verify everything I've just said.'

'There's no need, sir. Thank you for your time. I guess you were just unfortunate in the coincidence of it all. I mean… your accident happened before the death of Mr Milius and his girlfriend. You must understand how we needed to check all details out.'

They both stood as the detective gathered his notebook and pen.

'I do understand. I just hope you catch whoever did this. I did get injured by this careless incident, but I didn't know the guy. Even if I had, I'm sure I wouldn't have taken such a drastic action. I mean, look – I haven't even claimed compensation, or attempted to. What's done is done. Accidents happen all the time. I'm just grateful to be alive.'

As he ended his sentence, Robert noticed the figure of his wife in the entrance to the kitchen.

The detective sensed this and turned to look.

He walked over and reached his hand out. 'You must be Mrs Turner.'

'I sure am,' was the reply. 'I take it this is a pleasant visit, as my husband isn't ranting and raving in chains.'

DI Raymond laughed politely. 'Just checking on some details of his incident, that's all.'

Claire smiled. 'Well, it's nice to see things are followed through these days.'

The man turned to Robert. 'Thank you for your time, sir. I shall leave you two in peace and crack on with the day.'

'That's OK. I hope you find out what happened there. It's all very bizarre.'

The detective grinned and walked towards the front door. Claire walked behind and offered to open it for him. The man nodded and walked to his vehicle at the side of the road, without looking back.

Robert walked towards Claire. 'You're home early. Nice surprise, of course.'

She turned to face him. 'Yeah, well, I managed to catch up on everything. I thought I'd come home and sort my personal life out.'

Robert felt surprised at her sudden wish to rectify things. He wondered if she meant the same thing as he was thinking. His expression must've said it all.

She held his arm, led him to sit down in the lounge area and began to explain. 'You see – I realised I've been very self-centred lately. I've been out with Maria a lot, laid into work and house-work and not paid much attention to our relationship. I suddenly realised that I could lose you if I didn't start putting some effort into it.'

Robert still couldn't believe what he was hearing.

'I'm sorry about the other night. I didn't realise you'd cooked for me. I rushed to grab a few things after deciding on a last-minute drink with work colleagues. At the end of the night I knew you were pissed off with me as you'd already gone to bed, with a table full of food still sat there. I promised myself that I'd explain and make an effort to communicate more.'

Robert sat in silence as he felt his emotions fill his heart.

'Oh, Rob, I'm so sorry. Please say something. I hope I'm not too late to sort things out.'

It was almost said as if she was reading a speech.

This doesn't feel right, he thought. *It's like she wants something. Look at her eyes; they don't look meaningful.*

She was still talking and Robert suddenly realised he hadn't been listening to her words. His mind switched back to the conversation.

'Rob! Are you listening to me? We need to sort this out. I understand I've been distant and neglected everything lately. Please listen to me.'

Robert suddenly stood up and paced around the room slowly, as if he didn't care too much about the situation.

'Please talk to me! We haven't had chance to talk since that night. I think we need to sort it now. It's been my fault entirely. I can do the talking, but I need some sort of response.' Claire's frustration was now very evident. Her desperation to resolve the issue forced a tear.

That's more like it, he thought. *A bit of emotion… we're getting somewhere.*

Claire sat with her head in her hands. Tears were falling through the gaps in her fingers as she leant forward.

Robert's sympathy kicked in. He sat next to her and placed his arm around her shoulders. Claire instantly turned to tuck her head into his comforting chest. He allowed her a few moments of release before he spoke.

'I have a confession to make too,' he announced softly.

Claire held her position, but the whimpers halted to listen.

'With your recent behaviour, I couldn't help but wonder about the possibility of you having an affair.'

Her head sprung up to meet his eyes. 'What?'

Robert felt guilt for a moment, then realised his right to have suspected something. 'You must admit, darling: your actions have had reason for suspect.'

Her features were now firm, almost as if she had reason to turn the blame. They soon softened as she spoke. 'OK, Rob. I guess you had good reason to think that. The only thing I'm cross with is the whole trust thing. No matter what... I would never cheat on you. That's the most important thing I want you to remember.'

Robert looked at Claire with guilty eyes. 'We have a lot to talk about. First things first: I want to know why you've changed your behaviour recently. If it's something I've done, I could sort it out.'

Claire now felt scrutinised. Her cheeks changed to a deeper rose. 'I'm gonna be completely honest with you now, so please keep cool and calm.'

Robert raised an eyebrow in suspicion.

'I think it's been a few things, but when you work long hours, I get to be on my own a lot. I guess I became a little free-spirited. I thought I should ensure I get to do the things I enjoy and not just hang around waiting for you to come home. When you had time off, I guess I wasn't used to you being around and continued to be the same... you know... selfish, I guess.'

Robert's head hung in disappointment. 'I think I can under-stand where you're coming from. I do work a lot over long periods. I guess I've also been selfish by just assuming you'd hang around for me and wait for me no matter what.'

'We can work through this, you know – sort it out.' Claire sounded more positive.

'Yeah... tell you what. I'll cut down on my hours if you don't mind me plodding on at the same level. The money won't improve over the years, my aims will be average and I'll spend more time living my life... with you.'

Robert looked for a good response towards his humble offer, but Claire's expression didn't change. After a moment, cold words left her mouth.

'I think that's great. We can get on with things now... hopefully. I'll make an effort to communicate with you in future.'

Silence stood for what seemed a few minutes. Robert became confused over her tone of voice. It appeared to be devoid of any meaningful feeling.

'So that's that sorted, then,' he added.

'Yeah,' she said, as she remained in her hugging position.

The evening drew near as the couple sat in front of the blaring television. As their regular programme ended, Robert gazed at Claire's features and reached over to kiss her cheek.

She turned to him with a loving grin.

Robert reached over and leaned into Claire's body. She moved backwards for a comfortable position on the sofa. They kissed slowly and held each other's sides.

Robert suddenly stood and pulled her up by her hands. They continued to kiss and hold each other.

He lifted her while their lips still met, then carried her carefully up the stairs and into their bedroom. He then gently lowered her onto her back and unbuttoned her blouse.

They made love passionately in the light of a colourful lava lamp sat in the corner of the room.

Chapter Eighteen

The weekend had passed. Robert and Claire had spent most of it in bed, chatting and making love. Everything appeared to be great and revitalised.

It had now reached Monday morning and Robert dreaded his first day back to normality.

He rose to the sound of drilling outside. His eyes struggled to open fully as he climbed out of the side of the bed.

Claire looked very peaceful as she slept through the thundering noise.

Why do we have to bloody work? he thought, as he gazed at the beauty of his wife.

He reluctantly dressed and slowly walked down the stairs towards the kitchen. A bowl of cereal was quickly devoured.

Before he knew it, Robert had driven down the road and parked in the company car park. He drew one deep breath as he sat and looked up at the office block. The thought of work seemed to leave him cold as he visualised his wife sleeping at home.

How could I have allowed this stuff to take over everything? he asked himself.

He opened the car door and slowly stood.

'Hey, Rob!' a familiar voice shouted from the near distance.

He turned to see the curly, red-haired man from his department. 'Hi, Mark,' he responded to his call.

'How you doin'? We've missed you in the office. A whole loada shit's come in needing your expertise.'

'I'm sure that's an exaggeration, Mark. There are some top guys up there. But thanks for trying.'

'No! Seriously, I think you're gonna feel a bit pressured as soon as you get in the office.'

Mark grinned and walked away with his briefcase swinging wildly.

Robert hesitated. He didn't really fancy working as it was, without the instant pressures.

He gritted his teeth and walked through the car park, past the reception desk and into the lift. Sweat appeared on his forehead as he thought about the promise he'd made to Claire.

'I'll cut down my hours…' he'd said. But how the hell could he overcome the pressures and cut his hours down? He would have to see the boss as soon as he got in, he promised himself.

He reached the second floor and felt like everyone was watching him, as he approached his desk.

'Hey, Robert! How are ya? We've missed ya, man. It's been odd not seeing you sat there,' his colleague Ray said, sitting diagonally from him.

Robert examined his desk and saw that everything was pretty much the same as he'd left it. 'I'm fine, ta. I didn't wanna take all that time off. It's all the hassle you get from others forcing it on you.' He continued to scan his desk.

'Well, it's good to have you back. Y'know, sometimes others know better than you do at certain times.'

Robert grinned and sat down to turn his computer on. A tall figure appeared from the side. Robert looked up to see Julie Temple, the personal assistant to the managing director.

'Mr Turner, do you have a moment? Anthony would like to see you briefly.' She spoke in a soft, yet professional tone.

'Sure,' he replied, confused.

Robert walked behind Julie, out towards the lift area again. He looked at her curiously as she gazed at the lifts ahead.

'Don't worry.' She sensed his thoughts. 'It's all good.'

Robert looked away and thought about everything possible. *Maybe it's a welcome back thing; wants to show that he cares.*

They entered the lift and rose to the top floor. As they stepped out, Anthony was already waiting to greet them. 'Aah, Robert! Nice to see you in the flesh.'

'Likewise,' Robert replied, but instantly regretted the possibility of insulting the top man.

Anthony turned to walk. 'Follow me, Robert. I know you don't know this floor. We're just going to have a nice chat in my office.'

Robert felt very nervous now as he followed the sharp suit, walking a metre ahead of him.

They finally reached a large-windowed office at the far end of the floor. Its only contents were decorative plants, some strategically placed filing cabinets and a desk, which assumingly belonged to his personal assistant.

A central desk inside the office separated the managing director from the mere 'office worker'. Anthony took a seat and gestured to Robert to do the same opposite him. Julie slowly left the room.

'Now then, Robert... I've been looking at your work history with our company. Very impressive. In fact, I have to say, the best record within your department.'

Robert opened his mouth to speak some humble words when Anthony continued as if to prevent any interruptions.

'I heard about your recent incident... not good. I am sorry about that. Today's roads and all that...'

Robert opened his mouth in an attempt to downplay the event but was cut off again.

'Don't worry, Robert. I didn't bring you in for that. There are a few things I need to discuss with you; then I would like to make you a generous offer.'

'OK?' he managed to reply in curiosity.

'Well, this is the first time you've been away from work in the whole time you've been here. I've noticed you've worked consistently on many, many projects and had little reward other than what you may personally feel you've accomplished.' Anthony sat back in his chair and joined his fingers in front of him. 'While you were off, we had a few projects come in. People were recommending your assistance. When you weren't about, all hell broke loose. Delays were explained to various clients as a minor glitch in the system. Embarrassing for the company, you might imagine...'

Robert sat in silence. Feeling proud, he covered the smug feeling with a concerned frown.

Anthony continued. 'I didn't realise you were such an asset and that you were covering so much ground. You can understand my position surely, where members of staff cover their weaknesses to keep their records clean? I don't get to see the holes until justice finally prevails.'

Silence hung for a few seconds. Robert couldn't choose the right words to say. He didn't want to blow his own trumpet or knock his work colleagues' capabilities.

'So... Robert. Now knowing how important you are to the business, I'd like to lift you higher, but I'm not sure of your future intentions. Tell me a little about your ambitions relative to your career.'

Having to think quickly and feeling under the spotlight, Robert promptly responded. 'Well, obviously I don't want to be doing the same thing in five years or more, but I could never really see exactly where I was headed.'

I hope that keeps things open! he thought.

Anthony was obviously trying to read Robert's mind. He rubbed his chin with his fingertips and stared straight into the honest eyes.

'Mmm,' he finally responded. 'Well. I was considering head of your entire department for double your salary.'

It was like a probe. Robert saw the cash signs but couldn't shake the vision of Claire's eyes if he broke the news of more responsibility at work after their recent conversation.

Robert was silenced again as Anthony continued. 'However, I still can't help thinking you can do better than that. My problem is that I need you to continue your great work, but want to reward your specialist abilities.'

Robert suddenly had an idea that would work for both parties, given he'd been thrown a line.

'Well, I don't know if you'd agree with it, but I need to juggle my home life and work life, of course, and therefore have that good balance...' He nervously shuffled in his chair. 'I'm quite happy to do the same work, but with the benefits of working from home.'

Anthony didn't look as if that was the sort of negotiation he was planning.

Robert now felt a little silly and very self-conscious.

This is worse than going into the ring! he thought to himself, as he fiddled nervously with his fingers.

'Well, that wasn't quite what I was looking for. May I speak my mind, Robert, but not to intentionally offend?'

Robert nodded and grinned, now feeling more like the geek he'd always avoided being.

'I realise your great potential and know now that you are of great value to the company. For the time I've not realised this – all the great projects you have taken care of and accomplished – I feel this needs to be rewarded. Someone like you would be in great demand by other companies, so I would like to make you feel worthwhile and appreciated. Your idea is very humble, but I think you need to go home and think about what you would like. I am offering you an opportunity here.'

Anthony leaned forward to place more emphasis on the offer. 'Now I'm not aware of how ambitious you are as a person, as I've only been talking to you for a short while, but I am aware of your capabilities. So, go home, think hard, and come back to me when you've made your decision. I'd be quite happy with what you've come up with today, providing you continue your great work and accept at least twice the amount of money you're already on. We need to show our gratitude to you, my son.'

Robert felt as if he'd walked into a dream. What had he done that was so great?

Anthony looked down at some papers on the desk. 'Right, Robert; you have until next Monday to come and see me with your decision.' He looked through Robert and called his assistant. 'Miss Temple… please take Mr Turner to his desk now and see that he has everything he needs for work this week.'

Robert stood as Julie Temple gestured for him to follow her again.

He looked back to see the managing director studying his paperwork, as if the conversation hadn't even occurred. As they headed towards the lift area again, Robert felt that Julie might be more receptive to curious questions. 'So, does he really mean all that?'

Julie turned to face him. For a split second Robert suddenly realised how stunning her features actually were. Her brown eyes found his as she answered. 'He means every word, Mr Turner. He doesn't bring many people into his office, you know.'

They caught the lift and lowered to the second floor. They walked in silence to the entrance of the second floor. Robert found his nerve to speak again. 'It's OK: I can make it from here.' He chuckled slightly with nerves, following his sentence.

Julie looked as if she thought her help was unappreciated.

'Thank you for your help.' He reached his arm out in an offer to shake hands.

Julie responded and held his hand gently, barely moving the arm angle. Robert felt butterflies in his stomach as he noticed her beauty for a second time.

They gazed at each other briefly, and then she suddenly spoke. 'Is there anything I can get for you, Mr Turner?'

Yes please! he thought, as he temporarily lost all professional judgement.

'Er, no, I'm fine, thank you. I just need to get back into the swing of things,' he managed to reply.

Julie smiled and walked off toward the lifts. He watched her as her hips swayed in the most feminine way.

His rational thoughts suddenly returned to him as she disappeared into a lift. He shook his head and walked back in the direction of his desk.

Chapter Nineteen

A man knocked at the door. Matthew Carter walked over to greet his expected visitor.

The door opened to a tall, thickset man. His eyes were deep, his head shaven, the stubble indicating several unshaven days.

'What took you so goddam long?' Matthew shouted.

The man remained silent and walked into the lounge area uninvited.

Matthew looked through the front door, as if scanning for any nosy neighbours. He then closed the door and followed his guest to the same room.

The man stood in a steady stance, waiting for information.

'Well, Dino, I've tried and failed once before. The geek I used was just a kid. The job went undone. I need someone half-decent to come in and sort it out for me,' Matthew explained without going into boring detail.

There was a long pause before the man replied. 'I've gotta tell you straight, mate... I'm cool now, if you understand? I've got myself a lady... settled down. I was hopin' you'd give me something legit' to do, you know?'

Matthew looked hurt. 'You're my only hope now. You know how much I need this, don't ya?'

It seemed as if a nerve had been touched. 'I'm sorry, mate. I think you need to stick to yer tidy business. Why couldn't you've asked me this over the phone?'

Matthew's blood boiled with lack of patience. 'OK, you're wasting my time, then!' His head movement gestured him towards the front door.

His guest now had the expression of foe. He turned in disappointment and walked slowly to the corridor ahead. 'You know what, man? You're such an—'

His sentence ended abruptly, as the wire pulled into his fleshy neck.

'You little shit!'

The voice seemed deeper than ever now, close to his ear.

The victim could no longer speak as he fought to release the deep cut surrounding his last breath.

'You think I'd just let you walk away with your squeaky-clean attitude? You must've known I wouldn't have allowed an easy escape, with you knowing my plans. You're stupider than I thought. You deserve to die.' His voice was almost a whisper.

The body went limp and the weight was too much to hold by the thin wire. The flesh fell to the ground in a heavy thud as Matthew swiftly stood back.

The man now lay breathless in his own blood and saliva.

Matthew stood, now looking remorseful.

Chapter Twenty

'I'm telling you, man! We had some chemistry going on there!' Robert shouted as he hit the punch bag in front of him.

'I told you not to rush into marriage, didn't I?' was Richard's told-you-so comment, as he held the bag steady.

A few punches followed. 'I am married,' he puffed, 'so I shouldn't have those feelings, surely.'

'You know what they say, though: you can't help who you fall in love with.'

'Yeah. I think it may just be a lust thing... huh... so I mustn't even think about pursuing it.' He caught up with his breaths.

'I guess it'll only be a fantasy, then,' Richard ended.

Robert now looked disappointed. 'Yeah,' he replied as he continued to hit the bag several times before skipping gently on the spot to catch his breath again.

'You need to work on your cardio again, dude... you know they're about to set you up with your first pro opponent.'

Robert looked slightly shocked. 'You know... I've completely forgotten about the boxing future.' He stopped his movement and grabbed the punch bag to allow Richard a turn. 'I've got a new venture at work. At least, that's what I thinks' happening.'

Richard swung his arms before tucking into a few moves on the leather. 'What's happened, then?'

'Well, you know I was talking about this chick?' He didn't wait for a response. 'Well, she's the managing director's assistant. She took me to see the boss man. He basically offered me any job I want.'

'Jees!' Richard responded. 'That's cool!'

'Yep, but the problem is, I'm trying to sort me 'n' Claire out. We had this great chat and I agreed to cut my hours down. How can I cut my hours down if I take something bigger on?'

'Er, well, I guess you're gonna have to talk with her again.'

The bag swung slightly as Richard pounded the weight into Robert's middle.

'I guess. But then I said it could work if maybe I work from home quite a bit... but the boss won't take that as enough. He wants me to take double the pay at least, no matter what.'

'Wow! How cool is that!' Richard seemed very excited at the offer.

Silence reigned apparent for a few minutes as Richard pounded into the punch bag ahead without stopping for air. Robert wondered if he should be the one going up for the next big fight.

Richard stopped to shadow box, still facing the leather bag as he spoke. 'It seems as if you've gotta lot to think about, dude. You know, there's one thing I've learnt about life so far, and that's that you must do what you want to do. Whatever makes you happy, man.'

Robert thought the conversations with Richard always seemed to focus on his own issues. 'I'm sorry for going on about me all the time, Rich.'

'Yeah, well, that's what friends are for. Besides, it wasn't all that long ago that we were always talking about me and my problems.' Richard chuckled.

'You know, you're a good guy. I'm so lucky to have a buddy like you.' Robert suddenly realised.

Richard hit him on his upper arm. 'Come on, man. Let's hit the showers. I'm sure Claire'll be waiting for you at home.'

'She's working late tonight. That's the strange thing: she's allowed to work late!'

They walked down the corridor, talking and hitting each other's arms.

Chapter Twenty-one

The sea was rough; the boat rocked violently as Robert held Claire to keep her on board.

It was meant to be a nice summer's day. The boat sat too far into the ocean as it vigorously threw the couple side to side. Claire looked sinful as she walked to the heavier side of the speedboat.

'Claire! Wait!' Robert shouted.

She didn't appear to have heard him as she attempted to get the engine started.

Robert stood confused, when the boat jolted forward, knocking Robert backwards into the cold sea. He landed on his upper back, with his arms sprawled out to the side, to ease the collision with the water.

He struggled to keep his head above water as the waves crashed over him every few seconds.

Claire looked as if she was in control of the boat. She turned the vehicle to face Robert's direction.

He didn't question her skills, only waited for her rescue attempt.

As the boat approached, it slowed and spun slightly to enable a side-on view.

Robert continued to struggle with his water treading, hoping for a rope or arm to fall his way.

'Claire!' he cried impatiently as the boat rocked only a metre ahead of him.

Her face suddenly came into view over the side of the boat. Her eyes were dark and her lips thin, seemingly aggressive. Robert now realised he was alone. The sudden realisation left him feeling completely empty inside.

Her face disappeared again. Only a few seconds later, she returned to the boat side. A large stick was now visible. Robert thought there might've been hope.

The large stick, the size of a broom handle, came through the air too fast.

It was too late for him to avoid the severe blow to his crown.

His weight pulled him down below the surface. Still conscious, he was able to see Claire's satisfied expression through the clear seawater. Blood was now visible from the blow, as he felt a paralysing pull downward. Strange feelings passed through him: confusion, loneliness and fear.

A hand touched his shoulder as he sank deeper into the water. Robert turned to see his dad's face.

'Rob, You've gotta listen to me. Please hear me.'

'Dad? Wh—'

Robert sat bolt upright. He was covered in sweat. His breathing was heavy.

'Robert?' Claire asked, concerned.

He turned to see her physical features, realising what had happened. 'Uh, I just had this nasty dream!'

Claire pulled him back to the horizontal level of the bed and held him as he gradually calmed.

They lay in silence for a while. Robert couldn't shake the negative feelings.

It was only a dream he thought, *only a dream*!

The feelings lingered inside, leaving him immobile and thoughtful for a few hours. Claire had gone back to sleep, breathing calmly and innocently.

He watched her, wondering what the dream could have meant.

Her calm state eventually encouraged him to drop off to sleep.

Chapter Twenty-two

The new day brought better feelings, and Robert walked confidently into work. He started the day well, and worked through a few simple tasks until lunchtime.

As he grabbed his wallet and keys in an attempt to leave for his break, Julie Temple approached his desk.

'Good afternoon Mr Turner. I was just wondering if you'd had any thought on the previously discussed subject.' Her voice was smooth.

'Hi there,' he grinned nervously. 'I must be honest, I haven't thought about it too much yet.'

'You do realise the importance of this, don't you, Mr Turner?'

Robert felt slightly uncomfortable, wondering if the dream had warned him not to venture into the greener grass. He found Julie very attractive and felt like a school child in her presence. Luckily, he found an adult suggestion.

'Are you doing anything for lunch? Only it'd be nice to chat to someone close to the big boss. Maybe you could point me in the right direction… just a cup of coffee?'

Miss Temple now looked slightly uncomfortable. There were a few seconds of silence as she looked at the clipboard in her arm.

'Well, Mr Turner, I shouldn't—'

Robert interrupted her sentence. 'But you will, right?'

'Please don't put words in my mouth Mr Turner.'

Robert felt as if he'd really made a mess of things now.

She looked up with a more relaxed expression. 'My break is in twenty minutes. If you can meet me in the cafeteria downstairs in that time. I shall join you for a coffee and discussion on the matter.'

She's trying to keep it businesslike!

'OK. It's a date.' He thought he'd try his luck.

'A meeting, Mr Turner,' she confirmed.

He suddenly thought of Claire. 'Er, yes. Of course… I'd really appreciate the advice, miss.'

Damn! Wrong tone!

She walked off in silence. Robert sat there feeling slightly uncomfortable for a while, watching the clock.

Time passed quickly and he found himself nervously walking into the cafeteria. He noticed a waving arm in the distance. Miss Temple was keenly directing him over.

Robert walked over at a faster pace and sat directly opposite her.

'Do you want a drink?' he asked after suddenly noticing the empty table.

'Oh – yes, please. May I have a white coffee with one sugar?'

'Sure. I'll be back in just a tick.'

Robert returned shortly after with two hot drinks. The two made general conversation, then eventually discussed work.

'I just think you should aim higher. He was telling me you'd make a great teacher, someone who can pass the skills over to others members of staff. He sees the business improving immensely with that scenario.'

'Well, I don't mind that, but I don't want my life to consist of too many hours at work. In fact, just before the sudden announcement – if you wanna call it that – I was thinking about reducing my hours.'

Julie sat there in thought, biting her lower lip.

As she pondered, he gazed into her eyes, while attempting to hide his desire for her.

'Well, Robert...' she paused. 'May I call you that?'

'Sure.'

Rob will do, he thought.

'I think maybe you should suggest the training or teaching thing. You should only accept the specialised jobs, too – the ones that you know you can do a great job with.'

Robert looked up as he pondered over the idea, temporarily forgetting the distracting beauty across from him.

'You know what? That's a fantastic idea.'

'Can I also say... he thinks you're a huge asset to the company, so is willing to pay well over the odds for your continued employment.' Her eyebrows were now raised in excitement.

Robert felt bemused. 'This is just so weird. I've always plodded on at work. I knew I had more knowledge than the surrounding staff, but never boasted about it.'

'Well, he knows that. He also knows that you're not completely aware of your abilities compared to others. That means that he'll expect you to aim fairly low on the wage side of things. You have the power here though. Don't forget that.'

The conversation went well for a while. Both felt comfortable with each other's company.

'Oh shit! Have you noticed the time?' Robert suddenly shouted as he spotted the digits on his watch. Julie's face looked panic-stricken.

'Oh my god! He'll kill me! Is that the real time?'

'Yes! Let's get outta here!'

They both stood and walked briskly to the corridors ahead.

Both returned to their individual desks. Robert had enjoyed the brief time with Julie and found it difficult to concentrate on his work.

Why am I thinking like this? he wondered. *I must forget her and use the information she's given me to benefit my work.*

The afternoon passed by at a fast rate. Robert's mind was now decisive on the work issue. Work at home with the specialised projects; go to work to train others. Take double the pay! He decided the announcement would be made tomorrow morning.

Chapter Twenty-three

DI Raymond sat in his paper-cluttered office, working through the case of the Rose Wilkinson and Chris Milius' deaths.

Notes were spread all over the immediate area of the desk. The scribbled notes read:

Established the two were sexually involved;

Chris made phone calls to one person regularly;

Phone number called – linked to address;

Same road to address were reports of gun shots;

Owned vehicle seen at matched address to phone calls made;

Regular, large cash amounts to Mr Milius's account;

Drugs involved?

Mr Turner – wrong place, wrong time?

Large lorry involved in accident – found empty;

Mr Milius – fingerprints attached to lorry;

Gunshots to girl – right thigh and left temple;

One gunshot to man – forehead. All close range.

Studying the notes, he logged into his computer, pulled up a screen and typed in a case number. The details of Matthew Carter came to his sight. His full name, address, national insurance number and telephone number were displayed on the initial page. DI Raymond scrolled down to a page that demonstrated Mr Carter had no criminal record.

The detective pulled his pen out to scribble another note:

No criminal record attached to Matthew;

However, receiver of Chris's calls.

He pulled his mobile from his jacket pocket, dialled a number and held it to his ear.

'The murder of those kids... we've got a link. You got some time?' He listened for a moment.

'I need you look into the financial history of Mr Matthew Carter. I'll email you his details. I need to know his employment history, his taxes and how much cash is floating in and out of his accounts. Can you do that for me?' He looked down and scribbled some notes as he listened to the reply.

'OK, thanks. I'll need to go check him out in the meantime. Can you arrange that for me?'

He scribbled some more. 'Thanks, Craig. I'll speak to you later. Bye.'

He twiddled his pen and looked down at some evidential photos of the lorry incident. Thoughts went through his head as he scribbled some further notes:

Why trash a lorry?

Why drive it into the road?

No driver, just prints...

Robert and Claire were sat in their living room, sipping wine together in candlelight.

'We should do this more often.' Claire's eyes glowed in the dim lighting.

'I know. I wanted to talk to you properly, without the television blaring in the background.'

'Well, we've been talking for ages, Rob. You normally give in by now.' She gave a cheeky grin.

'I don't think about sex all the time, ya know!'

Claire felt slightly thoughtless when she noticed his meaningful expression. 'Sorry, babe. I guess this is really important to you.'

'Well, your opinion is very important to me, especially after the time we've had lately. I wanna keep things good if we can.' His eyes said everything to Claire.

'I think it's great. With more money we can live more

comfortably, do more things. And just to make things better, you're gonna be at home more. How can things be better than that, babe?'

Robert grinned and reached over to kiss her gently on the lips.

They continued to sip the wine from their glasses and talk peacefully about several things.

Time passed steadily and the couple decided to leave the drink and talk to head upstairs, when the telephone suddenly rang.

'Ignore it!' Claire shouted from halfway up the stairs.

'It could be an important call, honey…' Robert's face showed concern as he stared at the phone.

'It's eight o'clock. It'll probably be your mum wanting a chat. Don't let a call ruin our moment. Please!' Her expression was pleading.

The ring stopped just at that moment. The sudden silence made the decision.

'That's sorted it! Let's go!'

Robert chased Claire up the stairs to induce the previous excitement.

The phone suddenly began to ring again. They'd both stared at each other as they reached the landing area at the top of the stairs.

'Please just let it go,' Claire asked gently.

'How 'bout I just see who it is, then tell them we're just heading out the door, so can't chat?'

Claire backed down. 'OK, but make it quick!'

He hurried down the stairs to the phone and picked it up.

'Hello?'

There was silence.

'Hello?' he repeated.

Robert waited for a possible delayed response. Perhaps it was a bad signal from a mobile phone.

A whispery, distant voice said, 'Robby?'

Robert turned white and threw the phone onto the table, breaking the phone's cover.

Claire looked down from the top of the staircase. 'Rob? What the hell's going on?'

Robert looked blank as he stared directly at the broken phone.

'Rob!'

His silence disturbed her.

His hand shaking, he decided to lift the phone to his ear again. He heard muffled whispers, but no clear words.

He held the phone to his ear for a few more seconds, sweat breaking out on his forehead.

The distant whisper sounded again, this time broken. 'Rob-by.'

Robert turned to look at Claire as he listened intensely. She noticed his fearful face and ran down the stairs in sudden concern.

Claire pulled the phone from his ear and held it against hers. The crackle made no sense. To her ears it sounded like a very bad connection. She placed the phone down and looked at Robert. She hugged him around his waist.

'Rob, what is it? I heard a load of crackling… nothing… what's the matter?'

He stood in silence. Claire felt his body shake. It left her confused. She slowly led him up the stairs to the bedroom and sat him on the bed.

After a few minutes of pure confusion, Robert finally returned to reality. 'I'm s-sorry. It's just that I could swear the voice on the phone was… was… no, it couldn't have been. It was misinterpreted.'

Claire sat next to him on the edge of the bed. 'Rob, you're gonna have to talk to me. You're really freaking me out. Please explain what you think you heard. Please? You're frightening me now.'

Robert turned to face her and realised she was very nervous. 'Claire. Oh my god. I'm so sorry I frightened you. I just thought I heard something over the phone. Now that I look back, I realise it must've been my imagination.'

He reached for her hand and held it firmly. Looking into her eyes he found it hard to explain.

'Right. You're gonna think I've gone crazy, but you need to know – to explain my behaviour. I'm so sorry. It must have looked crazy!'

'Don't worry, Rob. Please just tell me what you thought you heard. I can't help you if you don't talk to me.'

He looked down and then raised his eyes to look at her.

'Well, I know your thoughts on this kind of thing, so I'm a bit wary.'

'Aah, come on, Rob! How much have we been through up to now? Huh? Nothing you say will change anything.'

Robert felt a little more at ease. 'OK. Well, I'll just come straight out with it then – my dad…'

He paused to look for a patronising expression. Claire gazed in confusion, waiting for him to continue.'

'My dad… He was the only person, ever, who called me Robby.'

Claire still sat patiently.

Robert continued nervously. 'I thought I heard my dad's voice calling me over the phone.'

Claire rolled her eyes in disbelief.

'I knew you wouldn't believe me!' Robert stood to leave the room.

Claire reached up and pulled his arm back towards the bed. 'I'm sorry. I can tell you haven't made it up, but you know I believe in rational explanations.'

'So you believe it could be possible?' Robert persisted.

'I believe you may have thought you heard something within the crackle noise. Sorry, Rob. I can't change my personal beliefs.'

Robert was lost in thought and didn't know how to respond. *Why does she have to be so rational*, he thought. *Open your mind, woman!*

Claire suddenly became very sympathetic. 'Let me get you a drink and give you a nice shoulder rub. That'll relax you. Then we can have some cuddles and go to sleep. Would that be nice?'

Robert understood her attempt to help in the situation. 'That'd be nice, hun.'

As she left the room, Robert sat in thought.

My dad's trying to communicate with me, he decided. *Who the hell do I see to get help on this subject?*

Chapter Twenty-four

Craig walked through the corridor leading to his boss's office. He knocked on the glass door.

An instant reply was shouted for him to enter.

'Hi, sir.' Craig attempted to show confidence.

DI Raymond sat behind his large desk, looking up at the officer in front of him. 'So, whatcha got, son?'

Craig raised a couple of A4 sheets to eye level. 'Well, sir, I noticed there have been regular cash deposits to Mr Carter's account. These look like legit BACS from a legit company. I checked the company out and everything's cool there. The only thing is, there is a lot of money drawn quite frequently. A lot... as in hundreds, sometimes thousands.'

DI Raymond prompted for more information. 'OK...?'

'Now, it looks as if he's worked for the same company for just over twenty years. His wage increases are reasonable, with possible promotions at times, which would seem normal for that length of time with a company.'

'OK, so you're saying everything appears to be normal other than the large withdrawals at regular intervals?' DI Raymond appeared thoughtful.

'Yes, sir. I do have to say, though, that some of the amounts withdrawn do match up with the amounts deposited into Mr Milius's account.'

DI Raymond sat, chewing his pen in concentration. He looked up at the young man. 'Fantastic! Right, I think we're gonna have to arrange a questioning of Mr Carter. I need to know about the connection with him and the couple. I need to know about his lifestyle – if he has many possessions; if he appears to travel a lot – basically see if there's an explanation for his expenditure. This needs to be done with discretion; you know the procedure... in fact, it'd be a lot better if we could get him into the station. I'll leave this for you to organise.' He looked up at Craig. 'May I say, great work. Thank you.'

Craig walked away from the office, a proud grin on his face.

Claire and Robert had woken together. Robert was soon dressed and ready to leave.

As he was about to kiss Claire goodbye, the telephone rang. Instantly, Robert jumped back in fright as he remembered the previous episode.

Claire grinned to comfort him and picked up the phone. 'Hello... oh hi... yes, he's here. Would you like to speak to him?' Claire passed the phone to Robert with a reassuring smile.

Who the hell could this be?

'Hello?' he asked curiously.

The voice was recognised this time, and Robert's relief was shown in his body language.

He allowed response time, but appeared to be discreet in the conversation, so as not to let Claire know what was being discussed.

'Yes. Well, if you'd like to arrange a time with that person, then that would be great.'

Claire frowned in curiosity.

He continued. 'OK. Yes, I do have a lot to discuss. Thank you, bye.'

Robert placed the phone down, noticing the severity of the broken cover.

Claire looked in his direction. 'Well? What did she want?'

He looked at her with worry but equal excitement. 'It was Sally, the one that had that strange thing happen... she said she's seen someone who's explained what happened that day, but that it also involves me.'

'So, what was the arrangement and the lots-to-discuss thing?'

'Well, she said that this person she saw needs to see me personally and that I would have a lot of relevant questions.'

'Oh. OK. So why were you trying to be secretive about what you were talking about?'

Robert sensed a bit of hostility in her voice. 'It's OK. It's just that you don't agree with the subject. I'm a bit embarrassed about following it through.'

'You mean the ghost stuff?'

Disappointment hit him suddenly. 'Yes. The ghost stuff... if you must know, she's had a spiritual medium talk to her and this medium would like to talk to me.'

Claire looked away in disgust, but decided not to get upset about the idea. 'Well, it's up to you. but don't take everything too seriously. I don't want to hear that you're gonna be a prince in a couple of years' time!'

'What? They're not that ridiculous... anyway, I've gotta go to work. Are you gonna give me a kiss or what?' He attempted to achieve an element of truce.

Claire looked over her shoulder at him and made an effort to walk over for a kiss. He gave her a cheeky kiss and made his way outside to the car.

He pondered over the words used by Sally.

I spoke with a medium, who says your involvement is strong and that she needs to see you urgently to pass on an important message.

He remembered her words. *I hope she comes back with a fast appointment*, he thought. *The suspense is killing me!*

As he walked to the car, he noticed that the day was warm, with a blue, cloudless sky. Excitement got the better of him. A medium! Answers at last.

Robert soon arrived at work. The office appeared to be fairly quiet that morning. This was his opportunity to find time to discuss his preferences for the future.

Walking through the corridors of the top floor, he remembered his way to the managing director's office.

Maybe I'm meant to make an appointment, he thought. He suddenly questioned his spontaneous actions.

Julie Temple stood in the distance, preparing the morning supply of drinks.

Business only! he reminded himself.

She sensed his approach and waved in his direction. Robert couldn't avoid his natural, nervous reaction. He felt his grin was going to give him away as he attempted to hide his feelings.

'Good morning,' he managed, as he grew closer.

'Morning,' she replied shyly.

'Is it, er, OK to just go ahead and knock on the boss' door?'

His professionalism vanished as his awkwardness directed his thoughts.

Julie grinned at his humility. 'Go ahead; he's just about settled in. He's been looking forward to hearing from you anyway.'

'Thanks,' he managed. 'I'll probably see you later.' There was no reply this time as he focused on the current subject. The office door was open, with the managing director sitting immediately ahead. 'Ah! Robert... please, take a seat.'

Robert was pleasantly surprised at the instant hospitality and quietly sat directly opposite.

'So...' Anthony continued. 'You returned promptly. Have you already decided?'

Robert grunted to clear his throat. 'Yes, sir, I thought long and hard and have consulted with my wife.'

'Very good, Robert. Please, call me Anthony.'

Yikes! That's too informal. Call me Rob! he thought as he tried to calm his mind. 'Well, er... Anthony... I have decided that training other staff on my specialist subjects would be the main role. I'd also like to continue with the more complicated challenges, but, if I may... do these at home. That way I achieve all of my goals and at the same time, keep the peace at home.'

Anthony sat in silence as he rubbed his chin. Robert felt uncomfortable. 'If, of course, that's OK with you, sir?' He worried that he may have dictated more than permitted.

'Well, Robert... I think that's fantastic, of course. I'm just thinking about the financial side of things. Have you considered the negotiable figure?'

Robert always felt uncomfortable when discussing money. 'Well, I thought that maybe I should leave that for you to decide, as I'm thinking you must have more of an idea than me.'

Anthony sat thoughtfully for a few minutes. Robert didn't know where to look.

'Well,' he finally returned. 'I think that maybe two and a half times your current salary?'

Robert grunted in surprise. 'Phew, that's very, very generous, sir... I mean Anthony.' *God, that must've sounded idiotic! He'll probably change his mind now*, thought Robert.

Anthony stood and reached his arm out for a handshake. Robert reciprocated but felt slightly confused.

'Robert, you can organise everything the way you like it. I trust you to train the competent and talented ones to be as good as you are. You may start your new role next week, with your new wage rise coming into effect as of today.'

Today? This guy must be desperate!

'Don't underestimate your capabilities, Robert. I'll be looking forward to the results.' Anthony spoke as if he had read Robert's thoughts.

'Thank you, sir.'

Anthony looked down at his paperwork again. 'Miss Temple? Could you please escort Mr Turner back to his desk?'

Robert felt odd with the abrupt dismissal after such an uplifting conversation. Miss Temple walked calmly by his side. They slowly approached his modest work area.

Chapter Twenty-five

Robert found himself in the gym after work.

I must get myself back in tip-top shape for the pro fights, he thought. *I will be pro! I will be!*

He concentrated on positive thoughts while skipping speedily to some loud background music. With the excitement of progress at work and home, he felt invigorated physically and found a vast amount of energy to train with.

The sweat ran through his hair and clothes as he skipped vigorously to the aggressive beat.

Then accidentally caught sight of the large wall clock in the distance.

'Shit!' He cursed himself when he realised how long he'd spent in the gym.

Robert managed some quick cool-down exercises, then rushed home in his sweaty clothes. As he walked through the front door, he attempted to creep upstairs.

'Robert!' Claire's voice didn't sound pleasant.

'Yes, hun?' he replied, hoping the kind response would diffuse any initial anger.

'Where are you?'

'I'm just cleaning myself up quickly… I went to the gym and got a little carried away… with time, I mean!' he explained from a distance

Claire's blood was boiling. 'It was your turn to make the meal tonight! I've ended up doing all the cleaning and cooking yet again! Don't tell me you're gonna cut your hours down at work but increase your hours in the gym!'

Robert now realised the intensity of her frustration and rushed down the stairs to find her.

He approached her red face and hugged her rigged body. 'God, hun, you must be really angry! Your body feels stiff with it!' He grinned.

She pushed him away. 'You think this is a joke? How many times are you going to promise things just to do the opposite? Do you know how annoying it's starting to get?'

Robert tried the sympathetic approach. 'Oh, my god. I'm so sorry. I've messed up again, haven't I?'

He changed his expression from the mischievous grin to the caring, concerned eyebrow raise.

If this doesn't work, I'm screwed, he thought.

'I'm so sorry… look – at work, I've changed everything to suit us. I'll make sure that everything's as we need it to be from now on.'

'Ok, but then what happens when you need to start training for your first pro fight? You'll be training full-time for months. What you gonna tell work then? I'm guessing you're gonna pursue the fighting, since you've been working out again.'

Robert hadn't even considered this and found himself surprised that Claire had.

'Well, no one's approached me about the pro stuff yet. I know I've signed up, but nothing's started yet. One thing at a time, huh?' He felt slightly awkward about his laid-back attitude.

'I'm sorry, Rob! I just think that we stumble over one block, but there's always one in the distance. I've been thinking a lot lately and realised that the fighting would be the next issue.'

Robert didn't know where this conversation was leading. 'I thought you were angry because I was late.'

'I was… I am… I've just had a lot of time to think while scrubbin' everything I can see.'

Robert tilted his head in sympathy. 'Come here, love. Everything's gonna be OK. It always is.'

They hugged for a short while, eventually agreeing to eat, then relax for the evening.

Their arguments got sillier by the day!

As they sat huddled together in silence, Robert couldn't help think about the plan to make arrangements with Sally's new acquaintance – the medium.

Chapter Twenty-six

Robert took advantage of work's telephone bill and called Sally during a quiet moment of his morning.

The phone was answered promptly. 'Oh, good morning, Sally.' He spoke quietly to hide his personal business from surrounding work colleagues.

'I've been thinking since our previous conversation and have been dying of curiosity since.' He scanned the office area as he listened to Sally's response. 'Uh, yes... would you mind?' He grabbed a pen and small piece of paper to scribble down a name and telephone number.

'Well, thank you very, very much... I shall call you just as soon as I've managed to see this lady.'

Robert placed the phone down and stared at his small note:

Mrs Jennifer Bentley. 336994 – call ASAP.

He placed it very carefully in his trouser pocket.

I'll call after lunch, he thought. Yikes! His nerves had kicked in already.

The day moved quickly. He looked at his watch, surprised to see that it had hit four o'clock in the afternoon.

I must make that call.

Julie Temple suddenly approached his work area. 'Good afternoon, Robert. I know it's a little late in the day and you haven't started your new job yet, but something urgent has just come in.' She pulled a small package from her clipboard and gently lowered it onto his desk. 'Is there any chance you could use some of your whizz-kid skills this afternoon?'

Robert suddenly saw his wife's face in his mind. 'I, er... really can't today. You see, the reason I chose the new plan was to resolve my personal life. If I work late tonight, I've had it.'

Julie noticed the worry in his eyes. 'OK, don't worry. I shall ask the client if they would mind hanging on until tomorrow. I'm sure they can wait just a few more hours.'

Robert felt weakened by her presence and didn't want to let her down. As she turned to walk away he couldn't resist the favour.

'Er, Miss Temple?' She turned in hope. 'I'll see what I can do. Don't worry about calling them. I shall leave the disk on your desk once it's complete.'

Robert cringed at his risky decision.

I'll call the medium lady in the morning, he thought, as he regretted the delay.

Matthew Carter sat in his car, which was parked in a business car park. Employees were slowly leaving their work premises and driving away. He regularly checked his watch to choose his best moment.

Eventually, workers filtered out in fewer numbers and the car park was beginning to look fairly bare.

Matthew waited a little longer and noticed the lights lowering on certain floors of the business centre ahead. He looked to the right to see two cars. One was particularly interesting to him.

Matthew looked up to see a very slim man leaving the main exit.

The man appeared frail in structure, with a guessed age-range of about fifty to fifty-five. His hair was very grey and wispy, with an attempted 'comb-over' style.

As he approached one of the cars to the right, Matthew stepped out of his and advanced towards the man

'Good afternoon, sir,' Matthew began. 'I'm sorry to bother you. I work in ops on the third floor and forgot to bring my pass out with me. I don't suppose you could lend me yours or come with me and vouch for me? It would be a huge help. Only, I'm not used to working during evening times and don't fancy driving another hour back home to get it. God knows what time I'd get home then.'

Matthew seemed sincere.

'I... I... I'm sorry, my son, but security wouldn't allow that sort of thing. You know how tight they are on the pass thing.' The man thought for a moment as he noticed the desperate face. 'I guess we could try... I'm sure they can call your boss or check you on the system.'

Matthew was hoping for an easier option. He looked to the ground in disappointment, then suddenly flung an arm out to grab the man's neck. The choke seemed to have immediate effect as the frail man turned an instant shade of pale grey.

'Just hand me your pass, shit face!' He tried not to shout so as to avoid attention.

The weak man reached inside his jacket pocket and pulled out a white card. There were no photos visible, only a couple of rows of digits.

Matthew didn't hesitate to grab it forcefully and hide it in his own jacket pocket.

In the single strong grasp, the man had fallen unconscious and suddenly dropped to the ground like a de-stringed puppet.

'Perfect.' Matthew was relieved to have dealt with such a feeble character.

He discreetly fumbled for the man's car keys and managed to place his unconscious body in the respective car.

Matthew began to walk towards the building ahead, while briefly looking back to check on the way the body sat in the car. He looked asleep and Matthew chuckled. His pace quickened.

As he walked, he placed some thin, black gloves over his hands. Looking down, he picked up a cigarette butt from the earlier smoke breaks. He placed this in his pocket.

He reached the front door and held the card over the magnetic box to the side of it. A click sounded, enabling him to push the main door open and enter the reception area. A guard looked up from the desk. 'Evening.' He greeted in assumption of legitimacy.

'Evening,' Matthew returned as he threw a polite grin. 'Would it be OK for me to pick up one of my disks from my desk? I shall only be a couple of minutes. Homework 'n' all that, ya know?'

'Sure. I don't normally see you during the evening. Must be important.'

Matthew sensed the probing. 'Well, I like to stick to the day work. All work and no play…'

The guard grinned and nodded. 'Yeah. You've got it right. I'd stick with that if I were you.'

Matthew knew this part of his plan was his biggest challenge and felt that the ease of the entry was too good to be true.

He found a drinks machine on his way through and commanded a white coffee with sugar. As the full cup automatically dropped, he placed some strong sedatives into it and stirred.

He spotted a cleaner with a light feather duster coming in his direction.

'Excuse me?' he said.

The cleaning lady responded with a questioning expression.

'I don't suppose you'd mind taking this to the guard, would you? I promised him a coffee, but suddenly have an urgent call to make.'

'Sure,' the cleaner shyly replied.

Matthew watched from a discreet area to ensure the job was done. Sure enough, the guard accepted the drink in pleasant surprise.

Matthew made his way to the second floor and entered the main work area. He recognised the face of the remaining worker and continued past to get to the far exit. Once there, he laughed under his breath.

He knew this was going to be easy.

Walking back to the entrance of the floor, he checked that the remaining person was occupied in his work. Matthew then moved out of view and removed the cigarette butt from his pocket and placed it lightly between his lips.

He lit this and drew the breath. He then deliberately placed the end on the floor and encouraged ignition with the carpet. After a few short minutes, a large flame had grown just inside the main entrance. Matthew moved back into the floor area and walked towards the rear exit again.

'This is going to be some show!'

As he stood by the fire exit, he viewed his wristwatch and checked for the smell of smoke. It seemed to take a while for anything to happen.

After a couple of minutes, Matthew noticed the worker suddenly run towards the fire exit.

Matthew quickly removed a mask from his jacket pocket and placed this over his face to hide his identity. He then pulled a small pistol from the back of his trouser belt.

The figure attempted to run past Matthew to escape the building.

'Ah ah ah! You aint going anywhere,' Matthew shouted, as he pointed the pistol in the man's direction.

'What?' The man was panicked.

'You're staying right here, Robert Turner. You either take a bullet and die, or you follow my commands.'

'Who the hell are you? What have I done to hurt you?' Robert nervously asked. His head was sweating as the adrenaline pumped through his body.

Suddenly, the loud, intermittent alarm hit the air. Robert's blood pumped faster than he could ever have imagined.

Matthew discretely viewed his wristwatch.

They both stood in silence. Matthew continued to aim the gun at Robert's middle.

Robert finally answered. 'OK. I'll do whatever you wish. What is it you want from me?'

Matthew grinned behind the mask. Everything was running as smoothly as he had previously planned in his head.

'Right, Mr Turner. Move over to that wall.' He gave a small shuffle of his pistol.

Robert reluctantly complied, wondering how fast the fire was spreading. The air was becoming warmer by the minute, but the smoke hadn't reached that end of the floor space. Flames were causing some distant crackling noises through the gaps of the alarm sounds.

Matthew suddenly kicked Robert between the legs, causing him to crumple in pain.

'Lean against the wall!' Matthew ordered.

Robert sat uncomfortably against the wall, holding his crotch.

Matthew pushed the gun into Robert's temple, and pulled a long piece of material from his pocket. As Matthew tied Robert's wrists and attached them to the heating pipe, Robert slowly began to recover from the blow

'Why are you doing this?' he asked. 'If you want something, just ask!'

Matthew finished his solid knot and paused to look at Robert. 'What you have, you won't give. I have to force it from you.'

Robert sat confused, trying to identify the man behind the mask.

Matthew roughly placed a large cloth into Robert's mouth and gagged him. He then dragged one of the department's large work desks over the top of Robert in an attempt to hide him.

Robert looked around him in panic, breathing heavily through his nose.

'Goodbye, Robert.'

Matthew briefly admired his work, then escaped through the fire exit.

He ran down the staircase and out of the building. Thinking quickly, he turned to get to the main reception area again. As he entered, he noticed the sleeping guard on the front desk.

Matthew ran over to find the camera system. He found it and ejected the tape from the recorder. Placing it in his jacket pocket, he turned to the guard's face and aimed his weapon. He stalled momentarily. *This time you live*, he thought.

Matthew looked at his watch again and ran from the building towards the car park. He could hear the emergency services' sirens in the distance. He hurriedly started his engine and drove off the work site onto the main road.

Chapter Twenty-seven

The fire had spread fast, with the smoke thick and heavy. The sound was unbearable. Crackling, thundering fire and smoke smothered the floor and air space, the fire alarm pounding sharply, as if it were alive, attempting to attract attention.

Robert instinctively knew the fire was nearing. The smoke filled his lungs and burnt his nose and throat. The only positive thing for him was that he was low enough to breathe some air.

All sorts of thoughts hit his mind together. Who was this man? What did he want?

More importantly, he worried for his wife and the consequences of his possible death.

He tried to bring his mind to the current problem and the chances of untying himself.

He struggled with some wrist and hand movements, but the tightness told him that this would be impossible. The man knew what he was doing.

Robert viewed the metal pipe to look for a weakness. His eyes stung in the smoky air, tears running in the heat and frustration.

I aint gonna make it!

He attempted to kick the piping, but this didn't have a positive effect. His breath was beginning to grow short. He felt his consciousness fade.

He knew he'd escaped a serious house fire before as a child, but couldn't remember much about it. Flashes of his past came to his mind; thoughts about the consequences of current events.

'Claire,' he whispered as his mind drifted.

Everything went blank.

As Matthew drove, he suddenly realised a flaw in his plan. 'Shit!'

He spun the car around and returned the short distance.

Matthew knew he could still complete his task, despite the fire brigade following his tail.

Running, he retraced his steps and noticed Robert unconscious on the ground. 'Perfect!' he shouted.

Covering his mouth and nose, he rushed to cut the material from Robert's wrists and placed it in his pocket. On turning to run, he realised an additional support to his plan.

Facing Robert again, Matthew walked over and moved his body into a comfortable position. Looking over at one of the work desks, he acquired a reference book and placed it in Robert's fingers.

The sirens had arrived.

'Time to go, my boy!' he shouted to himself. He began to run, a pleased grin on his face.

He approached the final exit on the ground floor.

Gingerly looking out, he checked to see where the fire-service people were. One team member was stood talking on the radio by the side of the vehicle.

'Shit!' Matthew whispered.

Looking around, he noticed some shrubbery leading to heavy bush behind.

Making sure the fire person was occupied, he quickly ran and jumped into the greenery, not noticing small cuts due to the sharp branches and thorns. He pulled himself through the thick bushes and dropped through the other side. He immediately looked about to see if anyone had noticed him. Luckily, no one was about. He had landed himself in a quiet piece of green, assumingly provided for the local residents.

Checking in his pocket, he pulled out his black wallet.

'Now I have to pay for your death, Robert,' he murmured under his breath. He decided to go for a local drink until the commotion had faded.

Chapter Twenty-eight

Claire sat at home. The temperature dropped as darkness enveloped the house.

Time to put on the lights, she thought. I can't believe my last moan didn't have any effect on that goddamn man!

She angrily threw some cushions into their rightful place as she pondered over Robert.

Not a man of his word! Still annoyed by his persistently poor timekeeping, she heavy handedly threw objects into their intended areas.

Time passed and Claire was wondering whether or not to call Robert, but then thought against it. She was tired of arguing with him over the same subjects.

It was now eight o'clock in the evening, which was even beyond Robert's standards.

Claire wondered if it was right to worry or to keep the angry thoughts. If he walked through the door at this very moment, she didn't want to encourage his actions with a concerned hug.

'Damn him!' she cursed, while walking towards the telephone.

She picked it up and dialled his work number. The line connected and rang continuously.

'Come on! Where are you, you little bugger?' She couldn't help shouting into the air.

With no answer, she decided to call his mobile phone.

She waited for an answer. The car was with him, so she'd have to make her own way if she decided to go out on a hunt.

Maybe he's driving and can't answer the phone, she convinced herself. *Oh, why do I care? He obviously doesn't. I'll give him 'till nine, then I'm calling his mother. She can do all the worrying then.*

Time passed and Claire had cleaned the kitchen to a state of spotlessness. She placed the floor mop against the wall and lifted the bucket of water to worktop level and poured the water down the sink.

The phone suddenly rang. As she headed towards it, she realised the darkness in the hall area and turned to switch the nearest light on. She held the phone to her ear.

'Hello?'

Claire paused with anger, expecting a lame excuse from her husband.

Her expression turned to shock and fright.

'He's in the hospital? He's only just come out!'

She placed the phone down and anxiously reached for a thin, cream jacket. Remembering she had no transport, she reached for the phone again.

'Richard? You're not going to believe this…' she calmly.

Chapter Twenty-nine

Robert sat comfortably on the hospital bed at a sixty-degree angle, watching the nurses rushing around competently. Everything was open-plan this time, only flimsy curtains to separate the beds.

A small oxygen tube sat across his face, with two linking tubes entering the entrance of his nostrils.

He looked around to notice that the lights were dim and that most patients were attempting to sleep.

I need to get outta here!

He was attempting to get up, when a recognisable face appeared.

'Robert!' Claire flung her arms around his neck. 'I was so worried! What on earth has happened this time?'

He grinned. 'Well, it's gonna sound crazy.'

Claire stood back and looked into his eyes.

'It's just smoke inhalation. I'll be out of here in no time. Hopefully!'

'Well, just wait for the clear before jumping the gun. In the meantime, please tell me what happened.'

Robert sat on the edge of the bed in an attempt to explain. 'You see, I got held up at work, but still planned on a reasonably early escape...'

Claire didn't seem to appreciate the opening statement.

'Er... anyway, suddenly there's a fire and I run for the fire exit, but there's this bloke stopping me! He forces me back with a gun, then ties me up to a pipe near the floor.'

Claire's expression became intense. Robert paused to look at Claire for consolation.

'This bloke knew my name. It was so surreal... anyway, apparently the fire brigade didn't find me initially. Ended up, this facilities man and his security guard see my legs sticking out from under a table upon inspection of the damage.'

Claire looked confused. 'Well, how come the fire brigade didn't see you?'

'I guess the bloke planned to kill me. He moved a table over me, so that I wouldn't be visible.'

The both looked at each other in silence for a few seconds. Claire appeared to be bemused, but then suddenly met his eyes again. 'Why would someone want to kill you, hun?'

Robert managed a shrug of his shoulders.

Claire suddenly said, 'Did you report this to the police?'

'Yup. They came over first thing and asked a whole load of questions. I don't think they believe my story though. My hands were untied and holding a book by the time I was found... the fire brigade reported that a careless cigarette caused the whole thing. The lame security guard missed all of it as he decided to get some sleep at the time.'

'What?' Claire seemed completely dazed by the information.

'Claire, hun... you do believe my story, don't you? Someone tried to kill me, then somehow made it look like an accident.'

Claire paused before answering. She nervously walked away without speaking and disappeared down a corridor.

'Claire? Claire!' Robert couldn't understand her bizarre behaviour.

I'm the goddam victim here, he thought in frustration.

He pulled his legs over to his original position on the bed and sat in disbelief.

'Hello, mate!' The familiar voice was like candy to his ears.

Robert looked up immediately to see his loyal friend. 'Rich!' His voice lifted.

'I just had Claire in tears, not knowing what to think. I sat her down and came over... she needed a ride...'

'No need to explain, my friend. It's good to see you.'

Robert patted the small seat beside him.

Richard sat and looked at his pal. 'So... this is weird, huh?'

'Yeah. Rich...' Robert didn't fancy explaining the scenario again. 'You know I trust you, don't you?'

Richard placed a hand on Robert's shoulder. 'Of course I know that, man! You can tell me anything – you know that. I love you no matter what, dude. We're brothers. Maybe not biological, but we're definitely brothers.' He let out an embarrassed chuckle at the end of his sentence.

'Cool. Well, I think someone's out to get me. In fact, *I know* someone's out to get me, but I don't know who. What the hell can I do? The police are doubting my story and my wife can't handle all this.'

Richard looked concerned. 'Sounds as if you're gonna have to explain all to Uncle Richy, man.'

Chapter Thirty

Claire sat in a waiting-room chair. She wiped the tears from her cheeks and looked about in all directions. After a moment she looked strong and determined.

Getting to her feet, she straightened her clothing and began to walk back in the direction of Robert's bed. As she approached, she noticed him and Richard whispering intensely.

Richard suddenly spun around to notice her. 'Claire?'

She faced Robert. 'Can I have the car keys? I have a few things to do, but can't do them without a car.'

Robert frowned. 'But the car's at work... and it's really late.'

'Well, maybe Richard could give me one final lift.'

Tension hit the air. The two men looked at each other. Claire held her hand out, determined.

'They're in the cupboard.' Robert nodded to the small cupboard at the side of the bed that held his personal belongings.

Claire knelt down and hurried to find them as Robert and Richard looked on in silence. She pulled them out and immediately placed them in her trouser pocket. Then she set off in the same direction she had come from.

'Claire!' Robert called, baffled.

It was almost as if she had become a robot on a mission.

Richard followed her with his eyes. 'She wants me to take her to your car, yet she's scrambled off. What d'ya want me to do, bro?'

Robert looked to his right and redirected his gaze at Richard. 'Can you maybe... take her, then watch her, without her realising?'

'You mean follow her?' Richard's eyes enlarged in disbelief.

'Just make sure she's safe. You don't need to see what she's up to behind closed doors. OK?'

Richard paused for thought. 'Sure... I guess that's OK. When you comin' out, anyway?'

'Just as soon as I can, dude.' Robert nodded after Claire.

Richard reached over and gave him a strong hug, then walked off in the same direction.

Robert moved to sit on the edge of the bed again and reached down into the cupboard to pull his jeans out. He pulled a note from the rear pocket and unfolded it to read:

Mrs Jennifer Bentley. 336994 – call ASAP.

A nurse passed. 'Excuse me, nurse?' She turned to attend to him. 'May I use a phone?

'Sure. I'll help you pull your apparatus along with you,' she smiled cheekily.

Rushing footsteps came towards them. 'Robert!' Richard breathed. 'I don't know where she is!'

Robert stood in shock. He looked at the nurse. 'Can I leave now? It's only smoke inhalation. I'm fine now.'

The nurse looked disappointed. 'You need a doctor to clear you. You're still attached to a tube.'

Her face looked very concerned.

He turned to face Richard again. 'OK. If you could get to your car and wait there for a while. If she doesn't show, then drive to my car and wait for her there. She's taken the keys, so she'll wanna take the car. If she doesn't show then get back to me.'

'How long do I wait?'

'Use your judgement. I trust you.'

The nurse was frowning. 'Is there anything I can help you with?'

Richard rushed off as Robert soothed her. 'Everything's fine. My wife's just a little upset right now. My buddy's just going to comfort her.'

The nurse, obviously not convinced, continued to assist Robert in his mobility.

Robert suddenly stopped. 'Hold on… what's the time?'

The nurse wondered, then consulted her wristwatch. 'It's, er, eleven thirty.'

'Oh my god. It's too late to make a phone call to a complete stranger, huh!'

He turned to face the nurse. 'You must think I'm nuts. I guess I should try to sleep, then attempt this again tomorrow.'

'Well, it has been a little traumatic for you and you should get your rest.'

'It's important, but it can wait,' he said softly.

The nurse smiled and walked away.

Robert waited a few minutes, then looked about the check for privacy. Once he knew he was alone, he carefully removed the tubes from his nostrils.

It's not safe here. He'll find me, he thought.

Grabbing his belongings, he left the ward with vigilance. Finding the main exit he noticed a taxi rank and head directly for it.

Matthew had found his way to the hospital. Scanning the large entrance he spotted a patrolling security officer and followed him into a small room. It looked empty upon entering. Pushing the officer into a wall by the throat, he barely had time to react. In a short time, the security officer lost consciousness and fell to the ground. Matthew swiftly and aggressively changed into the uniform.

He walked to a large central desk, catching the eye of the receptionist. *She'll fall for my charm...* He grinned and asked some appropriate questions.

Leaving the desk, he found the ward reported to be caring for Robert Turner. He walked up to the nurse and asked, 'Is everything OK here, nurse?'

The nurse jumped slightly by the sudden question in her ear.

'Hi, yes, everything is fine,' she replied.

'I heard some guy came in from a big fire...' he asked.

The nurse studied his eyes briefly, then replied, 'Yes, but we've just noticed he decided to discharge himself.'

Matthew huffed loudly and began to walk away. He could feel eyes on him as he retreated.

As he left, he pulled his mobile phone from his pocket and dialled a number. Placing the phone to his ear, he awaited a response.

'Ah, hi. I don't know if you already know, but... he's gone. He discharged himself. He aint here and they aint gonna tell me where he is!'

He allowed a reply, then spoke again. 'Goddamn man just won't die. I have to come up with something fresh again. Anyway, you know now. Do ya still wanna meet up tonight at the hotel?'

He listened to a longer response as he walked quickly out of the hospital and into the car park. He came to his car and opened the door.

'OK, I understand. I'll get things sorted as soon as I can, don't worry. Catch you later.'

He deactivated his phone and threw it on the passenger seat.

Watching the people walking in and out of the main hospital doors, he let out a large breath and hit the steering wheel with his palms. 'Argh!'

Chapter Thirty-one

Robert reached home after a brief taxi journey. He noticed the car on the drive, which confirmed Claire's safety in his own mind.

He was about to knock on the door when he paused at the sound of raised voices. Claire and Richard, arguing.

He placed his ear on the door, but could only hear muffled voices. The tones of the two people were distinct, but the words – incomprehensible.

He decided to go through a side gate, which led to the rear garden.

Creeping towards the back door, he looked through the glass, seeking confirmation.

Claire was throwing hand gestures as Richard reacted to her shouting.

Robert decided to intercept. He knocked on the back door, which in turn induced a sudden turn of both heads. Claire's colour drained as she appeared to force herself to walk towards the door to unlock it.

Both stood silently as Robert entered his home.

'Well, I guess we've all got some explaining to do,' he said.

Richard picked his car keys up, already walking away. 'I'll leave you guys to talk.'

'No!' Robert snapped. 'I wanna know what all that commotion was about.'

Richard faced Claire, then dropped his head in disappointment.

Claire started. 'Rich is just peed that I disappeared without a trace after you told him to look after me. I didn't know you asked him to do that. I just wanted to get away from everything for a while. Your story of someone trying to kill you was just a bit too much to accept in my mind... I mean, why would anyone want to kill you, of all people?'

Robert stood with a slight lean. He looked at his friend for confirmation.

Richard folded his arms, looking uncomfortable. 'I don't wanna argue with your wife, man. I was just so worried. She took so long to get here and I'd been searching the streets. When I spotted the car pulling up, I had to come and check she was actually Ok.'

Claire looked guilty now. 'I wasn't sure if it was safe to come home.'

Robert now had the bigger picture. 'OK, guys, I think we're all just a little stressed and tired. Let's just have a drink and relax for a bit.'

Richard frowned. 'She could have just told someone something…'

'Rich!' Robert interrupted. 'It's over. OK? We all need to chill out.'

They all stood in silence, as Robert prepared some hot drinks.

As they held the mugs in their hands, the awkwardness became intense.

'Aw, come on, guys. I should be the one that's annoyed. Someone tried burning me alive!' Robert stressed.

Richard finally backed down. 'I'm sorry, man. I just got so worried. You know I'm a man of my word. I didn't wanna let ya down, man.'

Claire placed her drink down on the worktop quite clumsily. 'I don't think you men can see the severity of this. It's not just a case of apologising to each other to make things OK. Someone nearly died here!' Claire's eyes began to well up. 'My husband was almost killed.'

She stormed out of the room and stomped up the staircase.

The two men were left to stare at each other in concern.

Richard suddenly spoke. 'I think I should really go, dude. You need to sort your wife out. You know where I am if you need me.'

Robert looked agreeable. 'Thanks, Rich.'

Richard gave him a questioning look. 'You did get the… thing… didn't you?'

Robert nodded with a small grin. 'You're a good mate.' He punched Richard on the arm and walked with him to the front door.

Chapter Thirty-two

DI Raymond and his colleague sat in an office, running through the puzzle of Matthew Carter and the link between Chris Milius and Robert Turner.

'So. He killed Chris Milius and he could possibly be after Robert Turner,' Craig summarised.

'Yes, but I can't see the motive!' was the reply.

Craig looked at the notes spread over the table. 'Matthew Carter's car was at the scene of the fire during Robert's incident. We came along to check for any suspicious evidence after Robert's report.'

'I think we definitely need to speak with this man. Don't you? It seems odd that it'd be a coincidence to have two links where Robert was linked to this… Matthew Carter. Don't worry about arranging this talk. Let's go now.' DI Raymond made the assertive decision.

They both grabbed their overcoats and headed for the vehicle sat just outside the main entrance. Craig took the wheel and tapped the address into the GPS. They had hit the road within a few seconds.

'I do wonder how people land themselves in these sorts of messes.' DI Raymond attempted to make conversation.

Craig glanced over in surprise. The two normally only discussed work when in the same confined space.

'Well, sir, I guess sometimes it's easy to do. I think even we, as police officers, get in some pickles at times.'

The detective rubbed his chin. 'Mmm, yeah. I know a lot of us have our home issues when working in the force.'

Craig wondered if he was probing for admissions.

The two sat in silence for a few moments.

'It's just 'around here.' He turned the vehicle into a long street with houses along one side and a large playing field opposite.

'Er, number fifteen…' Craig continued in hope of a bit of extra assistance.

Craig spotted the house and pulled up in a nice large parking area.

They pointed to Matthew's car in unison.

'Right,' DI Raymond said. 'I don't want to be complacent with this guy. He could be very dangerous. Be ready for any eventuality. OK?

'Yes, sir.' Craig suddenly felt nervous.

'In fact, if he answers the door, you hang behind and call for a back-up car just in case... Goddamn. Why didn't I think of that earlier?'

'Don't worry, sir. I'm sure it'll be fine if we just act cool.'

DI Raymond threw a surprised expression at him.

Too many thoughts were now hitting Craig's mind as they knocked on the door.

Rustling sounds were heard, followed by aggressive footsteps towards the front door.

The door opened. Matthew found himself looking at two men, holding detective identification cards at eye level.

'Hello, officers. What's this all about then?' asked Matthew, attempting to act surprised.

'May we come in?' Craig asked from the back.

'Sure. Will this take long? Only I'm heading out very shortly.'

Craig noticed a half-packed travel bag in the corridor.

'Hopefully not. We just need to follow up some leads,' DI Raymond answered professionally.

As they walked, Matthew gestured to them to take a seat. 'May I get you men a drink?'

'Yeah, tha—'

'No, thank you. We're on the road a lot today, so mustn't feel the need to stop, if you know what I mean.' DI Raymond pulled a notepad and small pen from a top pocket.

Matthew held a T-shirt in his hand and began folding it. He looked cool and calm.

'May we start with some questions on some people you may know...' Craig began.

DI Raymond heard Craig's question, but his voice became background noise as he noticed a recognisable face in a picture on a small table ahead. He stared at this, trying to work out where he had seen the lady before.

The talking continued in the distance as he thought.

Chapter Thirty-three

Robert sat in the bedroom. Claire was tearful, reluctantly filling a large bag of clothing. He felt as if the relationship was now beyond repair.

'So. You gonna tell me where you're going?'

'I just can't take it any more, Rob. I need to spend some time away. Maria said she'll put me up while I sort myself out.'

'What do you need to sort out without me? Can't we work through all of this?'

Claire looked back, screwing her eyes up in disbelief. 'How many times do you have to end up in hospital? How many more strange events are going to occur? And, to top it off, how much weirder are you gonna get? I mean, look at everything we've fought through recently. I need to go, so that you can sort yourself out, while I get some stress relief.'

'You think this is all my fault?' Robert instantly regretted the words he chose.

She aggressively threw a piece of clothing into the bag. 'It certainly seems that way. I don't know what you're involved in, but you have been acting very, very strangely. All I wanted was a lovely, normal marriage.'

Robert stood and walked over to her. He tried to console her by reaching for a hug.

She shrugged him off and folded the flaps of her bag to meet in the middle, while pulling the long zip across.

She walked away and down the stairs, leaving Robert dumbfounded in the bedroom.

I can't go to work tomorrow, he thought. *Not with all this crap.*

He pulled his mobile phone out from his pocket and selected the contact.

The front door slammed as he stood holding the phone to his ear.

The phone was answered promptly.

'Oh, hi, Julie.' He'd forgotten how coy he became with this lady.

The simple response from Julie changed his mood instantly. She had reacted in a sympathetic way on remembrance of the fire incident.

'I was just gonna say that I'm having a few problems at the moment and didn't know who to inform about it.'

He heard the kind response again, then continued. 'Yeah, I guess I need a bit longer to recover. Just a couple of days?'

It was such a pleasant change, hearing the kind words on each response.

She offered to meet him for lunch the following day for some time out and a friendly chat.

'Well, I don't think that'd be a good idea. You know what people are like.' He couldn't believe he turned her down.

He re-thought. 'Actually, if you're not too busy, it may help.'

He ended the conversation and returned the phone to his pocket.

Robert walked to the staircase and looked over the banister to see the bare hallway downstairs. He wasn't sure how he should feel. At the moment it was a sense of emptiness inside. Reaching for a note inside his trouser pocket, he urged himself to find comfort from the medium awaiting his call.

Chapter Thirty-four

It was a clear, crisp morning.

Robert had woken up to a positive feeling. A sense of power returned to his mind; he was ready to sort out life's problems.

He dressed in a sporty style and walked jauntily through the house. He grabbed a small bag containing the small gun and a bottle of water. Checking the contents, he closed this and threw it over his shoulder.

He walked through his back garden towards the shed. His pushbike was now in view.

Robert forced the bike through to the front of the house.

As he sat on his haunches, pumping some air into the tyres, he began thinking about Julie Temple. The plan for his day was a determined one. but Julie's voice in his head softened the aggression.

I can't think about her! I've got to think about my marriage!

He pumped the tyres even harder with his resolute thoughts.

Throwing the small pump onto the grass, he hurriedly jumped onto the bike and cycled up the street. Pushing hard with his legs, he leant forward to gather more momentum. The small bag sat solidly over the middle of his back.

He'd memorised the route to his destination. The street turnings were taken as if the circuit had been practised hundreds of times.

Sweat beads now became apparent. His legs were almost robotic as he continued at the same pace.

I need to go so that you can sort yourself out. He remembered the words used by Claire earlier.

I don't even know what the hell's going on! He thought, frowning.

The cycling was expected to take a while, and allowed his mind to work certain things out. Medium first, Julie for lunch, then possibly take Jack for a peaceful walk.

It seemed a short time of thinking when he suddenly noticed he'd reached the street intended.

Number 59... He scanned the house numbers. 45, 46, 47...

There we go! 59!

He jumped off his bike and adjusted his muscles to gentle walking. He could feel his hot, red face as he walked up a short path to the front door of a small house.

Taking a deep breath to recover from his exercise, he knocked gently on the door. A few seconds later, a short, elderly, grey-haired lady opened the door. She stood with a hunched posture. Her face held a polite smile, uncovering crooked, yellow-tinged teeth.

He overcame her appearance and opened his mouth to introduce himself.

The lady spoke for him. 'I'm Jennifer Bentley. Thank you for coming, Robert. I've been receiving a lot of messages for you that are... well... I should say come on in first, shouldn't I?'

The lady seemed excited to tell her story.

Robert stood in silence, wondering where to leave the bike.

Thinking quickly, he leant it against the front wall of the house. The lady didn't offer to place it anywhere else.

I hope she's more hospitable inside, he thought.

He walked into the house and closed the front door behind him.

Chapter Thirty-five

DI Raymond was tired of feeling a fool. Matthew Carter was obviously hiding something. Craig had thrown polite questions in connection with Robert Turner, but the man had a good front.

It was his turn to throw some 'bad-cop' questions in.

'So! Mr Carter. Could you tell me which company you work for, please?' He flicked his small notepad into action and clicked his pen.

Matthew stopped his small talk with Craig and turned to the detective.

'Excuse me?' His attitude turned defensive, his arms folded in disgust.

'We're just gathering information here, Mr Carter. Now then... I would like the details of the company you work for, please.' His assertiveness was mistaken for disrespect.

'Who the hell do you think you are? What are you accusing me of here anyway?' His face was now red.

Craig intercepted, hoping to defuse any difficult situations. 'We just wish for cooperation here, sir.'

Matthew turned to Craig and pointed. 'You're a nice guy... polite, considerate and respectful. Who is this complete tosser you work for?'

Craig stood as DI Raymond pulled out his handcuffs in readiness. 'Now then, Mr Carter. I advise you to keep calm and give us the information we require. You stepped over the line there, so I advise you sit down and answer the questions.'

Matthew met Craig in the aggressive stance. Their faces were close and challenging.

Matthew stepped back and sat in a small armchair opposite, his eyes still focused on Craig.

DI Raymond was impressed by his apprentice's work. He gave a lopsided grin, then turned to Matthew.

'Mr Carter...' he started.

Matthew turned his head slowly in the detective's direction. His expression was stern and undefeated.

'Now then. You and Robert Turner... I know there's a connection, so I'd appreciate it if you were just honest and didn't insult my intelligence.'

Craig cringed at the provocative words.

Matthew folded his arms and turned to Craig. 'You men come to my home, insult me, accuse me of something I haven't done! I invited you into my house, you've taken my hospitality, buttered me up, just to throw me into some made-up story about some guy I don't even know! Now then, you're gonna have to tell me about the complaints process because this shit has just cost you guys your jobs!'

DI Raymond stood and turned to face his colleague. 'Well, in that case, I think we should take you down to the station. If we're wrong about any of the connections we believe to be true, then we can direct you to the relevant department. You don't even know if we're accusing you of anything, which kind of tells me you're guilty of something.'

Matthew's face dropped in horror. He felt as if there was no other way than to act innocently and comply.

He stood to match the detective.

'OK. I'll come with you, but you have nothing. You're wasting your time.' His voice remained calm and submissive.

Craig stood and looked at the two men, wondering if the situation was genuine or if Matthew was leading them into a trap.

All three walked calmly towards the vehicle outside.

Craig watched Matthew cautiously.

Chapter Thirty-six

The lady sat at one end of the table with a small tape recorder in front of her hands.

Robert sat nervously opposite her, wondering about what happens during these sessions. He became aware of his small bag beside him and decided to move it comfortably between his feet.

'Right, then,' she started. 'I take it you've never had a reading?'

He looked at her eyes, noticing the friendliness. 'Er… no, ma'am. This is all new to me. I'm a little scared.'

She let out a quiet but confident giggle. 'You're fine there, Mr Turner. All you have to do is listen to the messages I pass on to you from your guides and loved ones from the other side. OK?'

Robert still felt uneducated on the subject, but was willing to sit and listen. 'OK, thank you.'

She wriggled in her chair to get comfortable. 'Right, Robert. I'm just going to be quiet for a couple of minutes as I say a few things in my mind and prepare myself for the messages. Don't feel uncomfortable about it. Just relax with me.' Robert didn't reply, but looked at her thoughtful expression.

'Now then. I may keep my eyes closed during most of the session. It's just the way I work. I may open my eyes at times for other reasons, but please just relax.'

Robert thought he should reply, but his dry throat left him whispering. 'OK.'

'Right, Robert. I have a man here. He's desperately been trying to get hold of you and wanted one of my previous clients to go to you, to bring you here.'

'Yes,' Robert replied politely, remembering Sally calling him.

'OK. She was pushed by this person's hand to stop something. It had to be done, as the procedure about to take place was totally unnecessary… totally wrong.'

This could be Sally's story so far, he thought.

The lady shuffled in her seat again. 'Robert, could you do me a favour and respond with a yes or no? There's no need to talk about anything though, don't worry. We can do that at the end.'

Robert had the feeling of old school days creep back into his mind – where his teaches demanded the 'yes or no ma'am' response. 'Sure,' he forced himself to reply.

'Right. I shall continue.'

Robert leant forward and gripped his hands together in front of him.

'This person I feel… is a father figure. No – it is actually your father,' she corrected herself.

Robert felt his nerves return.

'Has your father passed over?' She wanted confirmation.

Robert remained uncertain of his reasons for attending this meeting, but responded politely again.

'Yes.'

'Yes, it's definitely your father,' she continued.

Oh gawd, what am I doing here? he thought, as she wasn't impressing him so far.

'OK, Robert. This man, your father, is showing me boxing moves. As he's throwing his fists about, I noticed his fists are fairly large.'

Robert perked up at this comment. 'Yes, he did have large, strong hands.'

Oops. I should have stopped at the 'yes,' he remembered.

'OK. I'm now picking up that he's been trying to send messages across. He was the one that stopped Jack from getting hurt. The lady was just doing her job, but it was the wrong thing to do. The dog was innocent.'

Robert realised his initial judgement of this lady may have been wrong. His thoughts were now accompanied by adrenaline.

'OK, Robert. I need to backtrack a little and explain something before I go on.' Her eyes remained shut. 'When people say the Lord works in mysterious ways… well, I like to say that *life* likes to work in mysterious ways. I do believe in the god energy, but not everyone does. That's why I use the word "life".' She exaggerated the word.

'OK,' Robert said.

'Well, you see… this bad time you've had lately, isn't a bad time – it's a changing time. What you have now isn't right. This "bad" time will take you through to the right life that you call the "good times". You will have to get through some challenging moments. It may seem tough on you, but when you come through it, you'll see why it happened.'

Robert sat confused.

'This was your chosen path, so that you can appreciate the good by experiencing the bad.'

Robert listened and understood what she was trying to say.

She continued. 'You have it all, you see, Robert. You have the look, the talents and we are just here to learn lessons. What you have would naturally bring things to you quite easily, but life's all about learning, so you need to experience the learning process the same as everyone else. Everyone has their different challenges, which teaches them something about life that they need to learn.'

Robert began to understand but wanted to move on to the messages he was meant to receive.

She opened her eyes and noticed Robert looking a little bemused.

'Right. I shall move onto the important bits now. Please understand that your father wanted me to explain that to you before he continued.'

Can she read my mind? he wondered.

'So, he says that he's been trying to pass messages onto you. The first was to stop the pain of the loss of a loved creature. He has since been trying to tell you that you are in great danger.'

He instantly thought of the cheesy films he used to watch as a child. You are in great danger! Noticing an unchanged expression on the lady ahead, he realised how serious the words were.

'Rob… he's saying you need to stop your wife. Stop her!' Her voice now increased in volume.

Robert's adrenaline began to pump around his body again.

'What? She's only gone away for a break. We need to sort things out,' he added.

She shuffled in her chair. The sweat poured from her forehead, almost as if she was sat in a sauna.

'No, Robert. You need to stop her actions. It's not you she wants.'

He felt as if something had hit him in the chest. *This is bloody confusing*, he thought.

'You mean she wants someone else?'

The room went quiet as if he had broken the rules of the meeting. The silence was very uncomfortable. He wondered if the old lady had fallen asleep. Her eyelids looked sunken.

There was a sudden continuation. 'Robert. They have plans. They want everything. Even your life.'

What was she going on about!

Her head tilted to one side. 'She's going to take your life and your belongings.'

'What?' he asked, confused.

'Policies... policies. Change your policies, he's saying. She wants your policy.'

None of this was making any sense to Robert. He became lost for words, hoping she could elaborate on a few of the comments.

'OK, Robert... he's saying look back at recent events. Look back at everything you've been through recently. He's reminding you of a time when you went for a walk with your dog and you were confronted by a figure. This figure was your father. He tried warning you of danger, but the message didn't work. You see... nightmares, vivid visions... those sort of things. They are messages that may frighten you, but it's because you need to notice them and listen to them. How would we notice a gentle dream? We would just dismiss it, wouldn't we? I think he's been trying more and more with the severity of the messages.'

Robert tried piecing the events together. The figure in the park; Sally getting knocked over; the knockout in the ring and the dream about Claire drowning him. He also wondered about the incidents that nearly cost him his life.

'Do you have any questions so far?' she asked, opening her eyes.

'Yeah. There was a message I was given during a boxing match, but I can't remember what was said...'

The lady closed her eyes again and sat in silence for a couple of minutes. Robert wasn't sure if he should elaborate on the question or sit in silence. Luckily, the silence paid off. She began to speak again.

'He was warning you. You were at an unconscious state, so he was able to meet you on the same level.'

She paused a moment, then continued. 'This was one of his closer moves. He was hoping this message would've been taken straight away. He needed you to know that you couldn't waste time. The message was whispered in your ear. I'm struggling to work out what he said.'

The lady's eyebrows lowered in deep thought.

'Maybe I should regress you,' she suggested.

Yikes! This is scary enough, thought Robert.

He sat in hope that she could work the message out without having to delve into other methods.

'Life insurance!' she suddenly shouted. 'She's after your life insurance! There's someone else involved. They are both after your life insurance!'

Robert raised one eyebrow in shock and felt the blood drain from his face.

Denial hit him after a couple of minutes.

Surely not! How do I know if all this is real?

He sat with his head down, deep in thought.

The lady knew further convincing was needed. 'You know how dogs can sense things, Robert? Well, Jack was trying to tell you, too. Remember the incident with Claire?'

Robert wondered how this lady was getting this information so clearly. He thought back to the time his dog almost attacked his wife. He looked up at the lady, needing to know his answer.

'How do you know all of this?'

She looked directly at him. 'I'm sorry, Robert, I always assume people understand how this works. I receive messages from the spirits of people that have passed over to the other side. Your father is talking to me and I'm just repeating his words. He's been watching over you. I sometimes receive a visual scene. It's sometimes like a short video clip in my mind. In the case of your dog, I could see that he was just trying to protect you from the evils of your wife.' She suddenly shot a glance of guilt at Robert. 'I'm sorry if I'm speaking too bluntly.'

Robert decided that this could be genuine and stood to leave the house.

'I've gotta get back quickly. If it's true, I'll have to test it.' He threw the small bag over his shoulder.

She stood and looked very concerned. 'Please be careful. These people aren't doing things lightly.'

He pulled his wallet from his pocket and dropped thirty pounds on the table.

'Thank you, my friend. You've done your part. I must now remove the danger.'

He walked away from the table and outside to his bike. The lady hurried after him. 'Please be careful, Robert! It's best to think things through before jumping into the fire.'

He turned back as he threw his leg over the bike frame. 'Don't worry, ma'am. I have a whole cycle ride to fathom out my next move.'

He smiled at her to show his appreciation, then cycled speedily away.

Chapter Thirty-seven

Craig and Matthew were talking formally in the small office. DI Raymond could hear the words repeated in the discreet office behind.

Matthew kept his cool, innocent approach, leaving no clues to the questioning party.

DI Raymond sat comfortably, thinking about the aggressive moment in Matthew's home.

He's obviously guilty, he thought. *We just need an admission or concrete evidence. There has to be something.*

He sat, sipping a cup of coffee slowly. A thought suddenly popped up in his head.

The picture! That's Mrs Turner!

He jumped to his feet and slammed the coffee down.

Running to the office door, he wondered why the realisation hadn't hit him before.

'Craig!' he shouted, as he unlocked the door and walked in. 'Can you step aside just for a moment?'

Craig looked surprised, yet followed the instruction. He walked to one of the corners of the room, still facing Matthew.

'Right!' DI Raymond started. 'I have a question for you!'

Matthew shifted his eyes to Craig and back to DI Raymond. Leaning confidently over the desk, his face fairly close to Matthew, he asked, firmly and clearly, 'Mr Carter, how well do you know Claire Turner?'

Matthew tried to hide his sudden worry. 'I don't know who you're talking about.'

DI Raymond grinned. 'Well, Mr Carter. How, then, do you explain the picture sat right in front of my eyes during our house visit?'

Matthew looked very unsettled but he wasn't going to be defeated easily.

DI Raymond noticed a sudden movement, but didn't expect the blow that instantly threw him to the floor.

Matthew stood with the chair in his hands. The detective was lying unconsciousness on the ground. Craig stood in shock but quickly came to his senses. He looked at his superior, hurt on the ground, then realised he had no weapon other than a matching chair in front of him.

Craig lifted his hands. 'Matthew… there was no need to react with violence. There's always a better way to deal with things. You didn't even explain the connection with Mrs Turner. You've just made things a lot worse for yourself.'

Matthew didn't seem deterred by the words. He looked at the scared young man in front of him and knew the advantage of confidence would win his way out.

Craig tried again. 'Matthew? There are other offices throughout this building. This room is covered with cameras. You'll have no chance. I suggest you put the chair down and submit. It'd be a lot better than injuring two detectives and running, I can assure you.'

Matthew's eyes were dark and furious. 'Sit your arse down on that chair before I smash you in, too!'

Craig didn't respond to the demand. 'You're making the wrong move! Put the chair down and sit in it before everyone ploughs in here and pulls you down.'

He glanced his eyes across at the unconscious man again and noticed blood seeping from his mouth. He was out cold, but noticeably breathing.

Matthew stepped back, still holding the chair. Craig still stood fairly close to the corner, hoping the officers in the building would soon attend at the scene.

Matthew moved quickly. The chair was dropped as he exited the door, locking it behind him. He was very grateful for the carelessness of keys left in doors.

As he walked out, he noticed that everyone was only interested in their own affairs.

Once in the open, he ran faster than he'd ever run in his life. 'Stupid little village cop shop!'

Running into a local field, he hid behind a bush and sat down. Pulling his mobile phone from his pocket, he found Claire's number and called her.

'Claire! I've had it! The cops know what's going on! Do you still have the car? Take it to the house and get everything you can. Take him for all he has then come 'n' get me… hurry!'

He waited for her response, then replied. 'Baby, just get all the money from the joint account, grab some pieces and hide in our usual spot. I'll make it there in about an hour. You've gotta be quick! They're on to us! I know it!'

Chapter Thirty-eight

Robert managed to arrive at the lunch venue just on time. His sweat ran down his face and dripped onto his top. He spotted Julie walking towards him. She smiled, then looked concerned once she noticed his manner.

She approached him, noticing his heavy breathing. She grinned again. 'Robert, you didn't have to kill yourself to get here.'

He couldn't appreciate the humour and found a way to speak relatively calmly so as not to frighten her.

'Julie, I've got to sort something out at home. Do you mind if we do this again another time?'

She noticed his seriousness. 'Sure, Robert. Is there anything I can help you with?'

He thought for a moment. 'Actually, there is. Would you mind ringing the police station and telling them I may be putting my life at risk? I've discovered a connection with my wife and some murderer!'

Julie's face went white. 'What's going on? I don't mind calling them, but I don't understand what I'm reporting here.'

He turned his bike to face his new destination. 'Please, just tell them that Robert Turner is on his way home, but he may be in danger. Tell them a Mr Raymond knows about some previous near misses with my life recently. Please, Julie? I need some back-up.'

Julie looked panicked, but reluctantly nodded her head. She felt him look into her eyes and sensed a great affection. She dismissed this and thought it was probably a look of appreciation.

He cycled away wearily and slowly picked up the pace.

Julie stood worried, then remembered her task and hurriedly walked to find a phone.

As Robert cycled, he reminisced about the good days. Memories of Claire and himself going for long walks in the country, play-fighting in the snow, enjoying other people's company, spending days out at the beach, nights in the cinema…

How did it come to this? he couldn't help wonder.

Where's my sodding car?

His annoyance took control once he realised how hard he had been peddling just to go and tackle a situation he didn't create.

His legs were now becoming fairly tired, but luckily he was approaching his own road. The car was there!

As he cycled, he felt the weight of the small gun on his back. The water had been drunk on the journey, leaving just the one item. It was nice to have the comfort of the weapon.

He stopped the bike a couple of houses away from his and hid it in a neighbour's planted area. He removed the gun and placed it behind his back, under the elastic of his shorts, covering the remainder with his T-shirt.

The house was quiet, the front door half-open.

Robert crept up to the gap and carefully peered in. He walked towards the lounge area and noticed Claire was on her own, scrambling through the drawer that kept vital paperwork.

He didn't feel as if he could face her. This was very difficult for him to deal with. His wife was suddenly this villain he didn't know. He leant against the wall of the same room; she was completely unaware of his presence.

Suddenly, she must've sensed something, as she turned to see him. Her face dropped in shock. 'Rob! I thought you were at work.'

He stood firmly now. 'I thought you'd gone to Maria's to stay.'

She appeared to stumble for an explanation. 'Well, er, I had to come back to get my passport. We may go away for some sort of a break. I could do with one.'

Robert felt his anger rise. 'Oh… well poor old Claire needs a holiday. Everything's gotten on top of her.'

She sensed his anger and looked surprised. 'What the hell's wrong with you? I'm getting away for awhile. You're the one that's done this to me.'

Robert shook his head. 'Oh yeah! I forgot! I nearly died – twice! And my wife's been so supportive!'

Claire became nervous. She'd never seen this side of him. He'd always been the introverted, submissive type despite the regular sport of boxing. The thought of his potential actions in this frame of mind was terrifying. She noticed the veins on his forehead enlarge, almost as if he was about to convert into some sci-fi monster.

He walked in her direction, attempting to work out her intentions. Nothing obvious sprang out at him. but he noticed the fear in his wife. She'd promptly sprung backwards and looked as if she was about to make a run for it.

'You stay where you are!' he shouted, while closing the door to the room.

Claire made the mistake of glancing up at the antique clock that sat on the sideboard. Robert had seen her glance at the clock several times in the past, usually when she was in a rush to leave.

'So! Who are you about to meet, then?'

'I-I'm not meeting anyone.'

'I'm not stupid, Claire. I've lived with you for quite a while now. I know when you have a time limit.'

She sat against the wall in silence and worry over his unpredictable temper. 'I know you've never seen me like this,' he continued. 'You've never made me this angry, that's why! I know exactly what's been going on: I just want an admission from you. I want to see you admit the whole lot. I want you to explain why you're doing it and what prompted you in the first place!'

Claire looked terrified. Robert didn't feel any sympathy at this point, only anger for the pain he'd been through over the last few weeks.

She managed to speak weakly. 'I'm r-really sorry, Rob, for whatever you think I've done.'

'Why the guilty conscience, Claire? You know exactly what you've done, so stop pretending. Like I say, I know everything, so spill the beans!'

She wouldn't speak, but sat shaking against the wall, with her arms tucked underneath her armpits.

'Do you want me to tell you what I know? Will that encourage you? OK then. I know you've been seeing some dangerous man who's been working with you to pop me off, just so that you can run off into the sunset with this idiot. What I don't know is why. Why weren't you happy with a normal, comfortable life? I have enough money to support us, I have a good job... we had a good thing!'

Robert weakened with emotion and sat opposite her in disbelief.

Claire noticed the change and felt comfortable trying to explain. 'We were drifting. I began to hate you. I have this shitty job, then come home and you'd never be there.' She began to cry. 'I found this other person, who... who showed me care and attention.' Her voice began to rise in confidence as she expressed her frustrations. 'We planned this together. If we had your fancy life insurance, we'd be sorted for life without the threat of you hanging around.'

Claire became more confident and stood up to walk away.

Robert stood swiftly and leant against the door. 'You're not going anywhere until the police get here!'

She rushed back to the opposite wall in fear.

'I'm not gonna hurt you. That's something you should like about me if anything... I would never hurt you.'

Claire frowned in frustration. 'Why can't you let me go? The police obviously know about what's going on, so you have no fear of me attempting the same crime.'

'I can't do that. You see, your little boyfriend is very dangerous. He nearly killed me – twice! That's the attempts I know about anyway! And, I don't know where he is right now.'

Claire now had a guilty look on her face and looked about her for a way out.

'I'm not letting you outta here until the police arrive,' said Robert. 'You're not getting away with this.'

He walked towards her. 'You made love to me... you made love to me knowing what you were doing. What kind of sick person would do that?'

She moved sideways, against the wall, trying to avoid him.

She still thinks I'm gonna hurt her, he thought.

The door suddenly burst open.

'Police!' the man shouted as he ran into the room, swinging a gun between the two shocked characters.

Robert pushed his hands into the air. 'You finally got here! I need to fill you in on the story! She's been trying to kill me!'

'Both of you... keep your hands in the air where I can see them!'

Robert was now worried that he didn't have the evidence he required. The man seemed determined to control both of them. 'Turn and face the wall with your hands on your head. Now!'

A bit harsh, thought Robert. *She's the bad guy!*

They both turned cooperatively and placed their hands on their heads.

A sudden blow to Robert's lower back instantly forced him to collapse.

Catching a glimpse of his surroundings, he noticed Claire running off with this person.

Robert was completely devastated. *How could he have been so stupid! A copper... in plain clothes... and maybe not even be a real gun!*

He remembered his weapon but couldn't seem to move for a few minutes. He heard the familiar engine noise start outside.

Luckily, his movements returned. The pain was intense to start with, but adrenaline soon triumphed.

He stood and ran to the landline. He dialled a number. This was swiftly answered.

'Rich! I need yer bike! Quick!'

Richard didn't seem to understand the urgency.

Robert tried another method. 'My murderer's escaping with Claire!'

Richard must've dropped the phone in sudden realisation. Robert ran outside to see the car move off.

The heavy motorbike engine approached as the small car-engine noise faded into the distance.

That was quick, thought Robert. *Even for a neighbour!*

Richard flicked his head to motion Robert to jump on.

They sped off after the car.

Chapter Thirty-nine

Craig had already had the paramedics in to attend to his superior He had attempted to order the police helicopter, but in the meantime had sent the troops out in force on the hunt Radio messages were returning to him every few seconds.

'God damn arsehole!' he shouted while entering his own vehicle.

He drove back to Matthew's house in an attempt to find clues as to his whereabouts. As he approached the house, he screeched the tires into the parking spot.

Craig was angry. His boss and friend was seriously hurt.

Remembering his uselessness frustrated him, yet encouraged him to confront the situation aggressively.

He forced the front door open and walked inside, while fitting clear gloves over his hands.

His first task was to get hold of the photograph. He spotted it almost immediately and placed it in a clear bag he took from his pocket.

Throwing items across the rooms, he searched for anything helpful. The bedroom was very disorganised, with papers and clothing everywhere.

Craig checked most of the loose paper, but found these to be old bills and useless notes.

'Damn it!' His frustration grew.

He sat on the bed, but rose instantly when the phone rang.

Running towards the noise, he noticed a small table with a cordless phone sat tidily on top. He stumbled over the rubbish beneath him. His body lost balance and he fell, pulling the small table over with him. The phone fell but continued to ring.

'*Aaargh!*' He couldn't control his anger now.

From the floor, he picked the phone up and pressed the answer key. 'Yes?' he abruptly answered.

There was a strange, inaudible crackle, followed by the engaged tone.

'Bastard!' he cursed.

About to stand, he noticed a small black book, slightly larger than A5 size. It was Matthew's diary! He opened it.

'Yes!' he shouted in triumph.

As he stood, he realised he may not have found this diary if the rubbish hadn't knocked him over in the first place.

As he scanned through the pages, a radio message came through. It started crackly and unclear; the final few words that came through were clear: 'Five minutes away. I repeat... the chopper is five minutes away from take-off.'

Craig finally felt positive.

'Don't worry, boss. We'll get 'im for ya!' he shouted.

Chapter Forty

At first they thought they'd lost the car, but luckily the traffic had slowed it down, allowing the motorbike to catch up.

The two figures at the front were obviously worrying about the chase. The driver pushed Claire's head down below the passenger seat level.

Very thoughtful of him! Robert cursed in his mind.

'What now?' Richard shouted to Robert.

Robert realised there was no plan. The hasty chase was on instinct. He suddenly remembered the gun behind his back. It was like a car-chase film.

What has my life come to? he thought.

'Follow him till we get to a quiet road! I'll hit his tyre with a bullet!'

Richard turned uncomfortably, then remembered to concentrate on the bike.

Suddenly, the car took a chance and overtook the immediate traffic. It pulled into a gap ahead, just avoiding a head-on collision.

'Crazy twit!' Richard shouted while opening up the throttle to catch up.

The two vehicles sped on, staying a short distance apart, and ended up on a winding, country road.

This was Robert's opportunity to attempt his audacious move.

Carefully reaching for the gun, it was almost as if Richard had read his mind. The bike was suddenly very steady and cautious, yet still at a reasonable pace behind the racing car.

Robert held his position carefully and slowly aimed the gun in the direction of the right rear tire. He knew he couldn't get this wrong. He would have only one chance before the driver twigged what he was doing.

His youth came flooding back to him. Memories of the cadet force and fiddling with old weapons that were available at the time, all students competing to gain 'marksman of the month'.

His mind returned to the current task.

What am I doing? he wondered. *Right! Bite the bullet!* He couldn't help humouring himself.

BANG!

The gun went off; the car veered as it was struck.

'Yes!' Robert yelled.

Richard suddenly slammed on the bike brakes as he noticed the car was about to collide with a piece of shrubbery at the side of the road. Robert's weight was flung into the back of his friend. He suddenly realised he hadn't thought about the next move. Adrenaline ran through his body.

The car hit the shrubbery and sat silently in the small ditch before it. Richard managed to pull up behind it, but was uncertain about what to do next.

The two car occupants remained in the vehicle, below seat level.

What were they up to?

Richard and Robert cautiously climbed off the bike. Robert held the gun loosely by the side of his leg, remembering that the enemy had held a gun to his head only a few moments earlier.

They slowly approached the car. Both men felt their body hairs standing up in fear.

The car remained still, no movement inside.

'This is a trap,' Robert whispered.

'What shall we do?' Richard quietly replied.

'I've got the gun, so I'll creep up.'

'No. It's not safe, man. You don't know what he has planned. I've got my mobile; I'll give the police our location.' Richard sounded logical.

But Robert still felt the need for revenge. Richard could see the temptation in his eyes.

'Don't do it, man. You don't know what he's gonna do. Why are they just sat there?'

Richard tapped the emergency services' number into his phone.

'Should we crouch down or something?' asked Robert, uncertainly.

Richard let out a quiet chuckle while holding the phone to his ear.

The phone was answered swiftly. Richard asked for the police and was connected in less than a second. He heard his mobile phone number repeated to him, with a control officer speaking over the top, asking about the nature of the call.

Richard started, 'Hi. I'm here with Robert Turner. We need some assistance. We've kind of detained someone who—'

BANG!

Richard felt a heavy blow to the right side of his chest. He stood initially in confusion, then noticed the man pulling his arm back into the car, his hand holding a small gun.

A stunned Robert pulled Richard down to the floor, on the safe side of the motorbike. He placed his hand over the obvious wound. The blood was dark and seeped through the leather jacket that Richard wore.

'Give me your phone, Rich!' he shouted, thinking about the emergency call.

Richard remained silent and managed the task of handing the phone across.

Robert didn't waste any time and placed the phone over his ear. 'Hello?' His voice was shaking. 'Yes, we're on the A325, from the A324 side. We need the police and an ambulance! My friend's been shot in the chest.' He threw the phone to the side and concentrated on his friend.

The words hit Richard's ears and threw him into a state of panic.

Robert noticed the change in his friend. His breathing became heavy and laboured, his expression confused.

'Don't worry, Rich, they'll be here. They know where we are.' Robert held the pressure on the bullet wound.

Richard shut his eyes tightly and tried to take his mind off the growing pain in his chest. He concentrated on his breathing, which was slowly becoming more difficult. He looked at Robert and attempted to speak. A weak whisper encouraged Robert to move closer.

'Leave me here. Go get your revenge!' he ordered.

Robert looked across at the vehicle. 'They're screwed any way,

Rich. The police are on their way. They're trapped; they know they can't go anywhere.'

Richard gripped the top of Robert's T-shirt. 'Get some skin! You'll regret it if you don't lay at least one punch in!'

'Look, Rich, this is no time to think crazy. I need to keep the pressure on your wound. Besides. I'm not exactly an experienced gunfighter.'

The car door opened slightly. Robert turned after noticing the movement. He swiftly moved to lie flat, moving to Richard's level. He heard a click in the distance. Robert lifted his head slightly to catch sight of the man pulling back his arm, gun in hand.

He's run out of bullets!

Robert reached for his gun again and pulled it out with intent.

'That's it,' managed Richard.

Robert looked at his friend. His expression was encouraging. He held the gun tight and stood aggressively. A few seconds passed.

Suddenly, the distant sound of a helicopter hit everyone's ears, causing movement in the car ahead.

Robert realised any revenge had to be taken now. He hunched over slightly and ran cautiously towards the car, like a big cat stalking its prey.

He reached the boot of the car but kept his head lower than window level. Creeping low towards the driver's side, he decided to try opening the door, so carefully reached for the handle. The noise of the attempt gave the plan away, forcing him to alternative measures.

'Open the fucking door!' he shouted, both arms at full stretch, holding the gun with both hands.

The two victims looked as if they'd been caught in a mischievous act. Their faces changed to the expressions of startled rabbits.

Robert daringly tapped on the driver's window with the gun to remind the man to open the door.

The two remained motionless.

The man seemed to pluck up courage. 'You're not taking us, you little shit! You're gonna have to drag us out!'

Robert heard the helicopter approaching.

Bang! The glass of the window dropped like water, displaying two clear, shocked faces.

'You'll go down first, you twit!' Matthew yelled.

'Get out of the car!' Robert shouted.

'Fuck you! You're gonna have to kill me first!'

Stubborn bastard! Robert had decided on his next approach. He threw the gun across the road, into the hedge on the opposite side. 'Let's have it out! One on one! Come on! I deserve this. You took my wife.'

Matthew slowly opened the door and stepped out, keeping eye contact throughout.

Robert's mind went to the ring side. This was gonna be good. Maybe he could have a near-death experience! His aggression built.

Matthew closed the car door and turned to face his opponent.

THUD!

A punch landed on Matthew's chin before he could react. He found himself on one knee in a twisted position.

As Robert grinned with pleasure, he noticed the passenger door open and Claire pull herself out.

'Ooph!' Robert's air was forced from his lungs as a powerful blow landed in his guts.

He realised she'd distracted him and moved into a defensive position. Matthew threw some lousy punches, and Robert avoided them with ease.

Robert retaliated in a spare second and connected with a jab, a reverse punch, following through with a powerful uppercut. It was that final punch that released all aggression.

Blood spouted through the air as Matthew lost control of his faculties. His body was thrown backwards and into the car behind him. He then slipped downward into a slouched, seated position. His head fell forward over his chest.

You're playing my game now! Robert's fist clenched tighter with thoughts of pure brutality.

He began to throw punch after punch into the already disabled opponent. The head flew from side to side. Robert was so intent on hurting the man, but the intensity of his anger was suddenly halted by a forceful blow to his chest! It pushed him into the road, forcing him to lose his balance. A feeling of humiliation hit him as he fell to the ground, landing on his rear end.

What the hell? Robert looked up to see an almost-dead opponent still leaning against the car.

He couldn't understand where the push had come from.

'Robert! I saw him! I saw the man push you!'

Robert looked across to see a pain-ridden friend lying on one arm, watching the scene. His spare hand covered the wound to his chest.

Robert quickly stood. 'What man? He's pretty much dead. I must've lost my balance!'

'No! There was the man with a big hand! The one that must've pushed that Sally woman you told us about!'

Robert stood in amazement.

Why would my own dad push me? he thought. The answer came to his mind in an instant.

I'd done enough. I went too far!

He stood dazed for a few minutes.

Robert had become so engrossed in the immediate event that he hadn't noticed the helicopter hovering near. He couldn't understand how such a loud noise could've been missed.

Adrenaline, I guess, he told himself.

He looked up to see Claire running across the field, occasionally falling over a tuft of grass.

What a fool you look, he thought

As she ran further into the distance, he realised that any good feelings for her had completely vanished.

Turning to check on his friend, he watched as he noticed him reverting to the full lying position.

Sirens were now approaching from the distance.

Robert ran over to his friend to check his stability.

'Rob, you did it. I'm proud of ya, man. Claire's off the scene now and I'm almost done. Go get Jack and take him home.' He handed over a set of keys.

Robert knew the key set well: one for the bike... one for the car... one for the front door.

He held them to uphold Richard's wish. 'You'll be fine, man.' he said. 'They're comin' ta getcha.'

'I dunno, man, but if I don't make it, I know I'll be OK,' Richard grinned.

The emergency services arrived and took control of the scene. The area became crowded with uniforms and high-visibility jackets.

Chapter Forty-one

Three Weeks Later

'Yeah, well, they'll probably come out early for good behaviour,' Robert said down the phone. He allowed a brief response. 'Yeah, he's fine now. He'll be bragging about it in the gym before long. How many people can say they have a gunshot wound to the chest? Ha-ha... OK, Mum, I'll come 'n' see you tomorrow. We can catch up properly then. Bye.' He placed the phone down and stepped outside.

The 'For Sale' sign sat on the front lawn. Richard and Rachael stood together, admiring the freshly cut grass. Jack wandered about on an extendable lead, sniffing the new, juicy ground.

'Are you sure this is what you want?' Richard asked as he noticed his friend approaching.

Rachael hugged him carefully and felt a pull from Jack's lead as he ventured a bit too far.

'Yeah. This house brings back too many negative feelings. I need a new start. Besides, I'm only in the next village,' he added.

The three smiled and looked in the direction of the house.

A small blue car pulled up to the front of the house. Julie Temple stopped the engine and stepped out.

Robert felt his heart flutter.

'Ah well, man. We'll leave you to it.' Richard tapped his friend on the shoulder and gently encouraged Rachael to follow.

Robert hadn't even heard his friend's words as he stared at his hopeful future.

She approached. 'You've been quiet at work. I just wondered if you were ready for that lunch you owe me.'

Robert smiled and gave her a daring hug. His smile widened as he witnessed her obvious comfort. Jack suddenly noticed the visitor and ran over to greet her.

Robert looked down at the dog and noticed the friendly greeting.

'He likes you!'

'It seems that way.' She smiled, noticing the wagging tale.

This is a great sign, he thought.

Epilogue

Robert's new kitchen was wider and brighter. He walked to the door at the end, which led to the lounge area. He looked in to see Julie holding their child. Walking over, he sat to give the two a loving hug.

Robert's mother came through from the opposite entrance and sat to admire the family.

She watched as she remembered her husband hugging her and the baby during the horrific fire all those years ago. Her eyes began to well up.

Her son noticed her emotion. 'What's wrong, Mum?'

She smiled. 'Oh, don't worry, son. You just reminded me of your father… it's a good thing.'

He moved over to her and placed his arm over her shoulders. 'Don't worry, Mum. We're all a family now and I'll make sure I look after us all.'

His mother smiled again and tried to hide her surprise at the strong similarities with his father.

For Robert, this was his new life, the one he realised he'd fought for.

There were two lessons he'd learnt in his life so far. One was that sometimes great things don't always come easy.

The other was that his father was always watching over them.

Printed in Great Britain
by Amazon

26864090R00092